SINGLE MOTHER

A Selection of Recent Titles by Julie Ellis from Severn House

AVENGED

DEADLY OBSESSION

GENEVA RENDEZVOUS

THE ITALIAN AFFAIR

NINE DAYS TO KILL

NO GREATER LOVE

SECOND TIME AROUND

VANISHED

VILLA FONTAINE

WHEN THE SUMMER PEOPLE HAVE GONE

SINGLE MOTHER

Julie Ellis

This first world edition published in Great Britain 1999 by
SEVERN HOUSE PUBLISHERS LTD of
9–15 High Street, Sutton, Surrey SM1 1DF.
This first world edition published in the USA 1999 by
SEVERN HOUSE PUBLISHERS INC., of
595 Madison Avenue, New York, NY 10022.

British Library Cataloguing in Publication Data

Ellis, Julie, 1933-
    Single mother
    1.   Love stories
    I.   Title
    813.5'4 [F]

ISBN 0 7278 5434 8

Typeset by Palimpsest Book Production Ltd
Polmont, Stirlingshire, Scotland.
Printed and bound in Great Britain by
MPG Books Ltd, Bodmin, Cornwall.

One

Carol Evans stood on the deck of the small, perfect East Hampton house and gazed with a sense of momentary serenity at the glistening blue of the ocean. The sky devoid of clouds, the sun summer bright, though this was early May. The temperature such that she was comfortable in turquoise linen slacks that reflected the blue of her eyes and a matching cotton turtleneck.

"Larry, I'm so glad your client loaned us the house for the weekend." The house that he had designed, she remembered with pride. She lifted her lovely, delicately featured face to his. "I wish we didn't have to go back to the city now . . ."

"We could have more weekends like this." His dark eyes were somber, belying his smile. Their weekends were always contingent on Ronnie's plans since Carol was obsessively concerned about being at the apartment much of the weekends Ronnie was with her father. *Suppose they have a fight and she wants to come home?* was her rationale.

"If you'd let us," Larry said, "we could have so much more."

Carol tensed. He'd come into her life almost eighteen months ago. Within three months she had known she wished to spend the rest of her life with him – as he with her. They were two people running from themselves – until they ran into each other. Seven years ago Larry's wife and five-year-old son had died in a car crash. Nine years ago she had divorced Jason.

"Larry, you know the problem." She struggled for calm. "I'm not free to marry yet . . ." She'd never expected to wish for that again until Larry came into her life.

"Why must we wait until Ronnie is off to college?" he challenged. "Why won't you give her a chance to know me?" Fourteen-year-old Ronnie had encountered him only twice in all these months. To Ronnie he was a consultant at the magazine where her mother was Editorial Director. Carol contrived for them not to meet.

"She's so fragile, so vulnerable. The divorce was traumatic for her. I can't let her be hurt any more than she's already been hurt." Carol's throat tightened in frustration. "She adores Jason."

"Has she forgotten what a bastard he was to you?"

"She was only five when I divorced him," Carol protested. But Ronnie had seen so many ugly fights between them – when Jason was drunk or into drugs. "Thank God she doesn't remember." There'd been years of therapy, with constant battles to make Jason pay even half when she was struggling to survive on a minuscule salary. "I owe her. She's a child with only one full-time parent."

"But she adores her father because he produces CDs that hit the top of the charts," Larry said with distaste. "How much did he see of her until the last couple of years?" What had brought about this metamorphosis? Guilty conscience?

"It used to be maybe half a dozen times a year – holidays mostly, though he had visitation rights every other weekend." She'd been glad he hadn't taken advantage of those rights. "Now he tries to see her every other weekend. He's proud of her."

"You've broken your back raising her through these years." Larry was grim. "I hate to see you working so damn hard, depriving yourself of a life of your own."

He knew that even in those early, very rough years Jason had contributed only three hundred dollars a month in child support – and Carol had had to threaten to go to court to get that some months – at a time when his income was soaring. She'd left him with nothing except that child support, worked long hours in a boutique and gone to college at night to earn her degree. With her BA she went to work for Max at Encore Magazines – a sleazy firm even today. But Max offered a better salary than she would have received at one of the glamour magazines.

Working for Max had never been easy – the more he saw her to be capable of handling, the more he thrust on her shoulders. But she'd taken that – and his psychotic behavior – because she needed the pay check. She'd risen from editorial assistant to Editorial Director in record time. She'd had to scratch for every small raise, but she'd been able to move from a tenement on West 108th Street to a so-called luxury apartment in the East Twenties. Ronnie had the bedroom, and she slept on a convertible sofa in the living room. The therapist insisted Ronnie needed her privacy. When Ronnie was nine and five teenagers attacked her to steal her leather jacket – Jason's Christmas present – he came forth with tuition for a private school.

"Another short walk on the beach?" Larry's voice intruded. "It's such a gorgeous day. And it's still early."

Carol glanced uneasily at her watch. "I think we ought to leave now."

"I know." His voice was gentle yet she read disappointment in his eyes. "You want to be back at the apartment before Jason brings Ronnie home."

"Larry, you know how I feel about you . . ." *How would I survive if I lost him now?*

"I hate seeing you torn this way." He reached to pull her close.

"I can't let Ronnie down," Carol whispered, her face against his. "She's had such a rough time in her young life."

"Sssh." He brought her face to his for a gentle kiss. "Okay, we'll leave now."

Seated beside Larry in his 1998 Lexus, Carol dropped her head to his shoulder as they headed westward. How could she make him understand her compulsion to be in the apartment on the Sunday evenings when Ronnie was returning from a weekend with Jason? Was she being illogical?

Of course, Ronnie came home from school each day to an empty apartment. A latch-key kid, her mind taunted regularly. But most afternoons Ronnie was at Paul's apartment, playing games on Paul's computer, going with him when he walked Machiavelli, his huge, lovable Bernese mountain dog. And Paul's mother – a non-working widow with a substantial income – was always home when Paul returned from school.

Still, she could never shake away the guilt that *she*

wasn't in their apartment when Ronnie came home from school. In earlier years there'd been a sitter, but she'd always been nervous that the sitter wouldn't show. Then for a while there were after-school activities.

"I've scheduled my vacation for three weeks in August." Larry interrupted her introspection. "What about you?"

"I'll take mine in August, too," she said with a sudden brilliant smile. Jason planned on sending Ronnie to a camp in Switzerland this coming summer. Last year it had been Canada.

"Why don't we go off for a cruise in the Greek Isles?" Larry took one hand from the wheel at the red light to rest on hers. "It could be heaven." He knew about Ronnie's summer camp.

"I couldn't," she protested automatically. "I mean, suppose something happened to Ronnie? I have to be home – or close to home," she amended. Last summer Larry had rented a cottage for a month at Montauk. She'd told Ronnie she was going out there with Iris, gave her a phone number where she could be reached. But the Greek Isles? Out of the country? She was cold with alarm.

"It's late to be renting in the Hamptons," he warned. "People are already signing leases right after New Year's." Instinct told her he'd been nursing this Greek Isles deal for weeks, had waited for what he hoped was a propitious moment to bring it up. "I'll call that great real-estate broker in Montauk who got us the house last year on such short notice. Kathy Beckmann," he remembered.

"Larry, that would be lovely." She sighed in relief that he wasn't arguing further. "Montauk is wonderful." And Iris would cover for her again. Iris thought Larry was great.

5

Just south of Bridgehampton, with Route 27 single lane each way, they encountered stop-and-go traffic.

"An accident just ahead," Larry surmised while they sat idle. "We're still very early," he comforted Carol.

Jason often frightened her to death by bringing Ronnie home at an ungodly hour, after promising to be back by six so Ronnie could do her homework. She'd read him the riot act a couple of times of late, though she hated having Ronnie see them fight. She knew what it was to be torn between parents. Her father and mother had made her a pawn after their divorce, and she'd vowed that would never happen to Ronnie.

"Carol," Larry tried again while they sat in unmoving traffic, "why can't you give Ronnie a chance to accept me?"

"I've told you." Her voice was strained. "She'll hate you. She'd hate any man in my life other than Jason." *But I don't want to lose Larry.* "Ronnie's going out to dinner and the theater with Cindy and her mother on Friday evening," she cajoled. "She's sleeping over at Cindy's. She won't be home until at least noon on Saturday." She treasured these times with Larry.

"Kids today accept relationships," he reminded her. "So we can't get married yet, but let me at least have space in your life that doesn't have to be kept under wraps. I won't intrude on your lives, but we can see each other without all the charades."

"Ronnie wouldn't accept it. She's one of those adolescents who lives in a dream world. She's so wide-eyed and innocent. Even with the divorce, she expects me to be faithful to Jason. Deep in her heart she hopes we'll get

6

together again." Carol frowned at Larry's contemptuous grunt. "I know – Jason's always involved with some new vocalist. But in Ronnie's eyes, that's 'promoting his newest recording artist'."

"You don't suppose some fancy college would accept her for fall enrollment?" Larry made an effort at humor. "I'll pay the tab."

"Larry, let's don't talk about Ronnie." *But how much longer can I hold him when we have to fight for more than two or three hours together?* "Don't let's spoil this wonderful weekend." Ronnie thought – again – that she was with Iris at an East Hampton house owned by Iris's aunt. Bless Iris for being her cover on these precious, too infrequent occasions.

"I'll call Kathy Beckmann in Montauk. She was so good at finding us an available house last year at the last minute – maybe she can do her magic again."

"Oh Larry, that would be so good," she said again.

Larry focused on driving. The cars in the accident ahead had been moved from the road. It was too early in the year for the summer hassle, Carol consoled herself. Yet she was nervous about the time. One stalled car on the Long Island Expressway could delay them thirty or forty minutes. A wait at the Queens Midtown Tunnel could be costly. *I told Ronnie I'd be home by six.*

They encountered one long tie-up on the Expressway, a brief delay at the tunnel. As Larry turned down Second Avenue, Carol checked her watch again, frowned. Still, when they approached the apartment building where she and Ronnie had lived for almost six years it was just fourteen minutes past six o'clock.

She remembered that she would encounter another rent

increase for her apartment when she signed the new lease. But even so, having a rent-stabilized apartment at a time when New York rents were going through the roof was a source of constant relief. For Ronnie she'd pushed herself into what was, for her, an exorbitant rent. In the first years it had deprived her of lunch, decent clothes, and vacations.

Carol glanced up at the twelfth floor terrace that had wildly increased the rental rate on apartments in the building but provided her with a cherished escape. At the time she'd signed the first lease, it had been the only vacancy. Despite her fear of heights she relished walking out onto the privacy of the terrace, shutting the door behind her. This was her own small, private piece of earth.

Her face lit up. "Ronnie's home." She saw Ronnie's near waist-length sweep of dark, silken hair. "I hope she hasn't been worrying because I'm late."

She always sensed an odd hostility towards her each time Ronnie returned from a weekend with Jason. Yet, at intervals, Ronnie brought tears of pleasure from her by some unexpected sweetness. Carol's mind zeroed in on the time Ronnie had come down with a virus last winter. Poor baby, she'd been violently sick. Afterwards, with the bed changed and in fresh pajamas, Ronnie hugged her and said, 'Mommy, I love you'. That was worth all the headaches.

Still, there was something special between Ronnie and Jason with which she could never compete. Jason was the big record producer with his name constantly in *Billboard* and *Variety* and *Cashbox*, and the gossip columns. Ronnie was so proud of him, though it bothered her that her father moved from one attractive girl to another – always a girl half his age.

Larry manipulated the car into a parking space in front of the building. Involuntarily Carol's gaze returned to the terrace. Why was Ronnie climbing onto a chair? Oh, to hang that pot of geraniums. Heights never bothered Ronnie. Jason and Ronnie were alike in that. They were alike in so many ways.

All at once her heart was pounding. "What's Ronnie doing?" Her eyes were galvanized to the twelfth-floor terrace.

A scream rent the air, cut eerily into the noisy street sounds. "No! No! Don't!"

Ronnie was falling over the ledge.

"Oh my God!" Carol heard herself screaming, felt Larry's arms move protectively about her. "Oh my God, my God!"

Carol wrenched open the door of the car and stumbled the few feet to where Ronnie's body lay, face down. A clutter of people gathered about.

"She almost hit me," a white-faced elderly man sputtered. "I could have been killed, too!"

"Ronnie . . ." Carol whispered. "My baby. My baby . . ." She huddled over Ronnie, cradling her head.

"Call for an ambulance!" a man yelled to the doorman. "Maybe she's still alive!"

"Did you see where she fell from?" a woman shrieked. "Nobody could survive a fall like that!"

"Call the cops!" a man ordered in outrage. "Didn't you hear her? She was pushed!"

"Carol . . ." Larry was trying to pull her away from Ronnie's body. "Carol, there's nothing you can do."

Two

C arol lay back in the dusky blue, corduroy-covered
chair that matched the convertible sofa where she
slept at night. The blue was repeated in the Rya rug that
dominated the room and formed the geometric designs
on the green background of the drapes, closed tight now
against the terrace view. Larry watched solicitously while
Carol struggled to answer the questions the detective was
firing at her.

"Look, can't you give her a break?" Larry intervened
at last. "You know what she's been through." Thank God
the doctor in 12-J had been home to give her a sedative.

"We understand how rough this is." Lieutenant Jenkins,
the older of the two detectives, moved his stocky body to
the edge of the chair. His eyes were compassionate. "But
we have a case of murder here. Two witnesses heard her
cry out. The apartment door was wide open. We must
assume that someone pushed her, then ran."

"It's important to get as many of the facts as possible
early in the game," Detective Corelli, the lean, compact,
younger detective, pointed out, his face impassive.

"Carol has had all she can take for now," Larry insisted.

"What about the father?" Corelli asked. "When's he
showing?" His eyes were appraising.

"I phoned him. He's on his way over," Larry repeated. Thank God Jason would take care of the funeral details once the coroner released Ronnie's body. He was reliving in memory the horror of handling the myriad details of Betsy's and David's funeral seven years ago. He tensed at the ragged sound of the intercom in the dining area. Even in these circumstances the doorman was announcing guests. "That must be Evans now."

He crossed to the intercom, instructed the doorman to send Jason up. He felt an unexpected hostility at the prospect of coming face to face with Carol's ex-husband for the first time. He had seen photographs in magazine spreads. Jason courted publicity. As head of Merrimac Productions he had been profiled recently in *People*.

At thirty-nine Jason Evans was still handsome, though beginning to show signs of dissipation. He'd exploited a talent for picking superstars in the music field to its highest point. Ronnie had inherited his dark hair and brown eyes rather than Carol's fair hair and blue eyes, but her features were carbon copies of Carol's.

A cop went to the door to admit Jason. His eyes glazed, his face ashen, he strode into the room.

"What's this shit all about?" he demanded. Carol shuddered.

"Ronnie's dead." Larry repeated what he had said half an hour earlier on the phone. He had felt little compulsion to soften the blow. "Somebody pushed her off the terrace."

"Christ!" A vein throbbed in Jason's temple. "Who did it?"

"We don't know yet," Corelli told him.

11

"Where the hell were you?" he demanded of Carol. "Always pissing off if she was a minute later than six!"

"We were caught in traffic on the Long Island Expressway. There was a bad accident . . ." Carol's voice was barely audible.

"You should have been here!" Jason shot back. "You're her mother. Why weren't you here?"

"Ronnie is . . . Ronnie was fourteen years old." Larry battled an urge to smash in Jason's face. Close up this way he showed the signs of too many women, too much booze, too many drugs. "She didn't need a baby-sitter at that time of day." How dare he try to throw this on Carol!

"We'd like to ask you some questions, Mr Evans," Jenkins intervened. Larry sensed the detective's distaste for Ronnie's father. "We understand Ronnie was with you this weekend."

"Is it all right if I take Carol into the bedroom?" Larry asked. The air crackled with hostility between Jason and Carol – she didn't need that now. "The doctor gave her a sedative. She should sleep."

"Sure," Jenkins approved.

Larry helped Carol to her feet. With a supportive arm at her waist he led her into the bedroom, Ronnie's bedroom, that shrieked of her presence. The queen-sized bed she'd coaxed Carol into buying. A dozen stuffed animals nestled against the frilly pink pillow slips that matched the bedspread. Three photographs of her father – all shot in his recording studio – sat on the double white dresser. The super-expensive stereo system with two huge speakers against one wall. Jason's Christmas present two years ago.

Larry felt the convulsive shudder that darted through

Carol as Jason's voice rose to a frenzied pitch in the living room. "What kind of fiend would want to kill that sweet, beautiful child?"

Larry saw Carol's eyes cling to a pair of jeans that lay in a heap on the floor. "Those are the Calvin Klein jeans I bought for her birthday two months ago. Cindy had a pair and Ronnie was dying for them, too. Her birthday fell on Friday, on a weekend that she was to spend with Jason, so we celebrated the night before." Carol was talking compulsively. "When she went to Jason's apartment that weekend she was wearing the jeans. She said she wasn't out of them – except to sleep – for the whole weekend . . ."

It was late March, with a threat of snow in the air. In the master bedroom of Jason Evans's sprawling penthouse condo in the East Sixties Ronnie lay wide awake beneath a white satin down comforter in the king-sized bed. She always slept in the starkly modern, mirror-ceilinged master bedroom when she was here. Daddy slept in one of the two guest rooms. She was naked beneath the comforter because it made her feel sexy to go to bed without any clothes on. The Calvin Klein jeans she had worn to the apartment lay across the foot of the bed.

Daddy would be sure she was sleeping by now. They had been home an hour. She had soaked in a perfumed tub, and then she had got into bed. Daddy had come in to kiss her goodnight.

"You like that new outfit?" he had asked smugly.

"It's terrific." Mom didn't know about these clothes. They stayed here in Daddy's apartment, to be worn when she went out with him.

Her eyes moved to the beige, pure silk Calvin Klein pants and top set that must have cost six hundred dollars, and which lay across a glass-and-chrome chair, one pant leg trailing on the lush white carpet. With make-up and the clothes Daddy bought her – Calvin Klein, Armani, Escada – everybody he knew thought she was eighteen. They didn't know she was his daughter.

"Five feet six and reed-thin," he had said with satisfaction earlier tonight when she walked out to show off the new outfit. She had grown five inches in the last seven months. She had just enough bustline to wear the top open almost to the waist, with nothing underneath. "You've got the kind of body Calvin Klein designs for."

She adored walking into a restaurant or a club with Daddy and having everybody's eyes fasten on them. He was Jason Evans, the hottest music producer in the country. She knew about all the girl vocalists who were dying to sleep with him, sure he'd make them the next big star in the Merrimac Productions stable. He always knew what was just arriving in the music field. Everybody said that. She read *Billboard*, *Cashbox*, *Record World* and *Variety* religiously, cutting out every item that mentioned Jason Evans.

Mom would flip out if she knew about the clothes Daddy kept in the master bedroom for her to wear when she came over here. Their secret, she told herself complacently. Nine months ago he had started buying these way-out clothes for her. Not even Cindy's parents bought her clothes like these, and they were as rich as Daddy. Jason, she corrected herself, listening for sounds in the living room. She was supposed to call him Jason when they were outside. Everybody thought she was his newest woman.

This was her fourteenth birthday. She'd thought they would stay at Elaine's to close the place. At first she'd sulked when Daddy said they had to be home by midnight because he was auditioning a new vocalist. But she knew how spaced out musicians were. So this vocalist insisted she could only see him at night, so what? Daddy said she was going to be the biggest thing since Mariah Carey. Only nobody knew that yet except him.

She pulled herself up on one elbow. She heard the door open, then shut. The vocalist had arrived.

"Hey, Tiger, you look sensational! But you're late," she heard Jason chide. "I raced from Elaine's to get here on time."

"You said you needed time to get your kid to bed," a vibrant feminine voice with awesome carrying power scolded. "You took her to Elaine's?"

"Her birthday," he explained with a touch of indulgence. "It gave her a thrill. She's tucked away and sleeping now. Cutest little kid you ever saw," he boasted. "Looks just like her old man."

He didn't have to make it seem like she was six years old. Ronnie simmered with resentment. She ought to be at Elaine's now instead of holed up here. Daddy had told Mom he was taking her for dinner tonight at Windows on the World so she could see the fabulous view, and then tomorrow they were supposed to go ice-skating at Rockefeller Plaza. Mom really believed that shit.

Ronnie squinted, listening for sounds from the living room. Weren't they going into the studio? Daddy said

15

he had to listen to her tapes. He loved showing off the studio. He had broken through four rooms to set up the studio and control room. He bragged that he had over four hundred thousand dollars worth of equipment in there. Tax-deductible. A business expense.

A couple of times Daddy had recorded her on tape. She couldn't sing worth a damn! Why did it have to be that way? Daddy could make her a superstar if she could sing even a little bit.

Sometimes Daddy let her sit in on a recording session. She loved the excitement, the tension, the crazy characters Daddy gathered around him. She'd stay in the equipment-cluttered control room with Daddy and the sound engineer, alternately watching the control panel and staring through the glass divider into the studio. She felt so important, listening to Daddy snapping out orders. *'We need more body, Joe. Come on! What the hell's with the echo? Let's don't waste time!'*

No, Daddy wasn't taking that girl into the studio. He was messing around with the living room stereo. But he wasn't playing Tiger's tapes, it was that new British group he had just brought over from London. He was keeping the volume low so as not to awaken her.

"You'll come into the studio next week." Ronnie strained to hear the conversation in the living room. "Then we'll see how good you are."

"Honey, I'm the greatest," Tiger boasted. "Every way." Ronnie tried to visualize the vocalist with her father. She'd be good-looking. Tall. Campy clothes. She had that kind of voice.

They were so quiet. What were they doing? Ronnie

pushed away the comforter, sat hunched forward to listen. She could hear the tinkle of ice now. Daddy was fixing drinks.

"I don't really drink," Tiger warned. "It makes me so damn sleepy."

"What do you do for kicks?" Jason demanded. "Drugs? Sex?"

"I screw," Tiger said, her voice a challenge. "Like nobody you ever knew. With me it's a whole new dimension."

"Take off your clothes and prove it," Jason ordered.

"Any way you want it, baby," Tiger promised. "I'm the greatest talent you ever met. On my back or before a mike."

Ronnie covered her ears. Damn that bitch! If it wasn't for her, Daddy and she would be at Elaine's. Or maybe they would have gone over to that new club he talked about. Why did Mom have to divorce him? Then he wouldn't be running around with creeps like that girl out there. What did she look like? She sounded *old*. Thirty, maybe.

"Honey, that thing ought to be insured by Lloyds of London," Tiger said, her voice eloquent with admiration.

"It's all yours, baby. For tonight."

Ronnie lay back against the pillows, pulled the comforter over her head. Tears filled her eyes. Her throat was tight with anguish. *Daddy rushed home from Elaine's so he could be with that hooker. That Tiger whore.*

17

Three

C arol stirred into wakefulness. For a merciful few moments the horror of the evening remained sequestered in the cavern of her mind. And then memory rode over her like a tidal wave. *She was lying here in Ronnie's bed.* She clenched her eyes tight, lay immobile. It hadn't happened. It was all a terrible nightmare. But truth was ruthless. A moan of pain escaped her.

"Would you like some coffee?" Larry asked gently and her eyes fluttered open.

"No," she rejected, but he was walking to the bed anyway, coffee mug in hand. She was here in Ronnie's room, where Ronnie would never be again. All at once she was shivering despite the warmth of the evening.

"The cops are gone, Carol. Would you like to go back into the living room?" He knew what it was doing to her to be here in Ronnie's bedroom.

"Yes," she whispered, pulled herself up, swung her legs to the floor. She wasn't here – this was a shell. She had died with Ronnie.

"Drink your coffee first," Larry ordered. He sat beside her on the edge of the bed.

"Larry, how am I going to live through this?" She lifted her eyes to his.

"You'll hurt like hell, but you'll survive. I've been there, Carol."

Now Carol remembered how Larry had waited at the airport for his wife to pick him up after a business trip, to learn hours later that she and their son had died instantly when a tractor trailer jackknifed across a highway. But they had not been viciously murdered.

"Larry, who could have killed her? It couldn't have been a robbery – nothing's missing. And Ronnie knew never to open the door to a stranger." Fresh pain rolled over her. "We have two locks on the door. The security in this building is great. The service entrance is always locked. So is the door to the garage. Nobody comes up without being announced." *Who would want to kill my baby?*

"The police have a rough case," Larry conceded.

"I have to know who killed her!" Carol was trembling. "Maybe one of Jason's spaced-out friends. Jason uses people so – and then he discards them. Like the woman who backed him in the record business years ago. When he had milked her dry of money he dropped her. 'You're old and ugly, who needs you?' he told me he'd said to her. Mrs Sheraton was a sixty-two-year-old widow looking for affection. She invested a fortune in Merrimac Productions."

"You don't think she killed Ronnie?" Larry reproached.

Carol flinched. "No. Mrs Sheraton killed herself the night Jason told her he was through with her. Jason's done terrible things to people."

"The police will follow up every lead," Larry reassured. His face softened. "Lieutenant Jenkins feels he has a special stake here. He has a fourteen-year-old daughter. He knows how he'd feel if anything happened to her."

"If the police don't find that fiend, then I'll spend the rest of my life and every cent I can raise tracking him down!" Carol closed her eyes in anguish. "If we hadn't been held up on the Long Island Expressway I would have been here. It would never have happened. My fault, Larry! I wasn't here for her."

"Stop blaming yourself," Larry commanded. He took the still-full coffee mug from her hand and drew her to her feet. "I'm going out to the kitchen to make us scrambled eggs and toast. Neither of us ate dinner. You go in the bathroom, shower and get into your nightclothes. I'll call you when the chow's ready."

"You'll stay with me?" She couldn't bear being alone tonight.

"I'm staying," Larry soothed.

Over the late supper, which she ate at Larry's insistence, Carol talked about Jason. Much of what she told Larry he already knew. Some she had kept locked up within her for years.

"Jason was a battered child. His father walked out when he was three. For years his mother – an alcoholic – beat him regularly, until he was big enough to hit back. He still has scars on his body from her."

"That's rough," Larry agreed. "But that doesn't give him a license to spend the rest of his life battering everybody else."

"He never touched Ronnie." Carol was defensive. "He only hit me once, when Ronnie was a baby. He cried when I threatened to leave him. He swore he'd never hit me again."

"Not physically," Larry amended dryly. "He had other ways."

"I was crazy about him in those early days. He had the kind of charisma that kept everybody hanging around him. We met in my junior year at college. He was twenty-four but only a sophomore because he'd dropped out after his freshman year. He'd wandered around the country, working at all sorts of jobs. In the spring of his sophomore year he dropped out again. That same spring my grandmother died. I've told you about her – she raised me from the time I was eight. Jason was hanging around the campus even though he'd dropped out. I clung to him. We were married that summer. Two years later Ronnie was born. We broke up when she was four, divorced when she was five."

"It's amazing the marriage lasted that long."

"We headed for New York right after the wedding. Jason was sure he had a great career ahead of him in music. At that point he wasn't sure just what it'd be, but even then he had an instinct about talent. The first year he worked for an agent who booked night club acts. Then he put together a singing group, managed that. I worked in a boutique until Ronnie was born. We weren't seeing much money, but we didn't need a lot then. We had a cheap studio in the East Village and a beat-up car that constantly broke down."

"Jason's making up for that now."

"Everything started to change when Jason bought a song from a musician who wanted bus fare home. He had the song arranged for his singing group. This was a period when independent record companies were bursting out all over, making it big. Jason raised money to start Merrimac Records – and that one song started him on the road up."

Larry wanted her to talk, she realized. It was a catharsis,

he thought. "By the time Ronnie was two we had a house in Connecticut. Two years later it was a bigger house with a pool and sauna. I hated suburbia. I was alone so much. In those days Jason was always on the road. I was stuck out there without a cent of cash, just yards of charge plates. I didn't even have money to go into a fast-food place for lunch. I had to charge gas for the car. That's the way Jason wanted it. And then he'd burst into the house with his entourage. They'd stay for days – drinking, doing drugs, having indiscriminate sex when they were drunk or spaced out. I'd take Ronnie and stay at a motel." With an air of exhaustion Carol leaned back in the gaily cushioned oak captain's chair that was one of a pair that flanked a small, circular matching table. "Why am I so full of recriminations now? That's long past."

"Pack a bag and move over to my place," Larry suggested on impulse.

She flinched. "I have to stay here – where I lived with Ronnie." Her voice broke. "Larry, how do I go on?"

"You're a survivor, Carol." Larry's eyes were stern.

"I'll survive because I have to see this . . . this *monster* who killed my baby pay for his crime. I've never believed in capital punishment. You know that, Larry? But right now, this minute, I want to see him strapped in the electric chair. I want to see him burn."

"You need to sleep for a while. The detectives will be coming back to ask more questions," Larry warned. "They're scratching for a lead."

"I'll do anything I can to help them," Carol swore. "But stay with me, Larry."

On Wednesday morning – the day Ronnie was to be buried

– Larry awoke minutes before six a.m. His sleep had been broken at frequent intervals. Ronnie's death had brought back the horror of arriving at JFK with the expectation of being met by his wife and son, only to discover three hours later that they'd been killed. He knew Carol's pain. He shared it.

He glanced with a surge of tenderness at Carol's sleeping form. So much anguish lay ahead of her. Let him, somehow, help her through it. She survived each day and night in a fog induced by medication. He hadn't left the apartment since this nightmare had begun. He phoned his office at intervals, called to confer with clients.

Thank God Jason had taken on the responsibility of arranging for the funeral. A limousine would arrive later in the morning to drive them to the funeral home for the service there, then out to the cemetery in Westchester County. Jason hadn't bothered to call. An office assistant had informed them of the day's schedule.

For the past two days Larry had talked to Carol's horrified friends and co-workers who phoned to offer sympathy. Yesterday – at Carol's insistence – he'd arranged for the two locks on the door to be changed. She was fearful that the murderer would return.

He left the sofa bed, debated about showering yet. Would the noise awaken Carol? Probably not, he surmised – she was sleeping under heavy sedation. Standing beneath the hot pounding shower spray he remembered his own reaction to tragedy. Carol mustn't be allowed to throw herself into work, to push aside all semblance of a personal life as he had done. Until he'd met her at that architectural conference almost eighteen months ago – she'd been covering it for a new magazine Max

Julie Ellis

had dreamt up – he'd thought his life was over except for work.

"Larry?" A frightened outcry carried into the bathroom. "Larry?"

"I'm in the shower," he called back, reaching to turn off the water. "It's early, honey."

But Carol wasn't worried about the time. She'd awakened alone in bed and she was frightened. Larry reached for one of the large, fluffy bath towels that hung on a rack and, still dripping water, hurried out into the living room.

"I woke up and you weren't there!" Carol huddled at the edge of the bed, her eyes reflecting terror.

"It's all right. I'm here," he soothed then chuckled. "Dripping water all over the rug."

She gazed at the window, the drapes drawn tight. "I think it's raining . . ."

"According to the weather report it should be stopping any moment." He stood by the bed and reached for her hand. "As long as you're awake, why don't you go in and shower? I'll make breakfast for us."

Carol closed her eyes in pain. "I keep thinking I'll wake up and find I've been having a nightmare." But in four hours they'd be in the funeral home listening to the service for Ronnie.

"Into the shower," he ordered and pulled her to her feet.

"I don't own a black dress," she whispered. "I didn't think about that till now."

"Ronnie wouldn't want you to wear black," he insisted. "But it's a cold morning – wear something warm."

Right on schedule the doorman called up to say that the

limousine was waiting. Per doctor's orders Carol had taken her morning pill ten minutes earlier. Holding her hand tightly in his, Larry led her from the apartment and downstairs to the waiting limousine.

At the funeral home a cluster of stunned classmates and teachers from Ronnie's school were already there. Larry held Carol's hand while people came forward to offer condolences. For Larry it was a replay of an earlier nightmare. Lieutenant Jenkins, his face somber and – at unwary moments – angry, sat close to the back. Larry suspected he was there as much in sympathy as to watch for any indication that the murderer was among the mourners.

A wisp of a girl about Ronnie's age came forward and flung her arms about Carol. "Mrs Evans, I can't believe it," she sobbed. "We were going shopping today at Bloomie's. My mom gave me my birthday check this morning. How could anybody do that to Ronnie?"

Larry realized this was Cindy Weinberg, Ronnie's best friend. And he recognized fourteen-year-old Paul Martin, who lived in an apartment on the floor above with his widowed mother. Paul came forward and pulled Carol to his tall, slight figure with an urgency that expressed his grief without words.

Mrs Martin had sent down a roast beef with her housekeeper Monday evening and a platter of cookies yesterday afternoon. She hadn't come to the service. Ronnie and Paul had been classmates, taking the bus to school together each day, Larry recalled, until this year when his mother had moved him into an all-boys school. Paul had adored Ronnie, Carol said, though there had never been a boy-girl relationship between them: '*Ronnie wasn't ready for that – in some ways she was young for her years. Paul would come downstairs to help her with her homework, or to cram with her when she was panicking just before an exam.'*

It was Paul Martin, Larry recalled, who had helped Carol with the flower boxes out on the terrace. She'd said Paul could make anything grow. How much a part of Carol's life he'd become, Larry mused – yet he was always outside the pale. Ronnie was not to know their real relationship.

After the service, in a depressing drizzle, Carol and Larry returned to the limousine waiting for them. Not a word had passed between Carol and Jason at the funeral home – but that was just as well, Larry thought with relief. Carol cringed before the accusations in his eyes. His earlier words were burnt into her brain: '*You should have been there. You're her mother. Why weren't you there?*'

Larry halted the driver when he saw Cindy Weinberg and Paul Martin hurrying towards the limousine. Two frightened kids coming face to face with reality, he thought compassionately. He lowered the window as they reached the limousine.

"Could we . . . could we go with you to the cemetery?" Paul asked while Cindy clung to his arm.

"Of course," Carol rushed to reply, and Larry opened the door for them.

At the cemetery a small group clustered about the grave site. At one side Jason stood, grim and angry, surrounded by a small entourage from his recording company. At the other side were Carol and Larry, flanked by Cindy and Paul, along with a pair of teachers from Ronnie's school.

26

Larry was curious about a tall, spare woman in black, her face white and strained, who stood at a distance. Shabbily dressed, she was somewhere in her sixties.

When the burial was over, Larry prodded Cindy and Paul to join Carol and himself on the walk back to the waiting limousine. He was about to ask Carol about the identity of the woman who was still standing at a distance but seemed reluctant to leave when Jason's voice cut through the silence. "What the hell are you doing here?"

Larry's arm tightened about Carol's shoulders as she turned to face the cringing woman.

"Jason's mother," Carol whispered.

"She was my only grandchild." His mother's voice was unsteady.

"It should have been you who was murdered," he said with calculated brutality. "Why don't you commit suicide?"

Jason's mother turned and fled while the others present gaped in shock.

"Did you know her?" Larry asked Carol – touched by the woman's forlornness, her pained reaction to Jason's ugly words.

"I saw her only four times in my life," Carol whispered. "Each time Jason made it clear his mother was not welcome in his home. I've spoken with her over the phone a dozen times each year. I never told Jason. She just wanted to know about her granddaughter. She was an alcoholic during Jason's growing-up years, but she said she hasn't had a drink since Jason was seventeen. I sent her snapshots now and then. Each year she sent Ronnie a small birthday present with a card that just said 'Happy Birthday from a friend'."

There was little conversation on the drive back into the city – each of them was absorbed in memories of happier times. At the apartment a group of classmates huddled in the corner of the living room. Carol's close friend Iris, a forty-nine-year-old divorcée who lived in the building and wrote erotic paperback romance novels, had come in during the funeral to set up a buffet luncheon. Paul's mother was out in the kitchenette preparing coffee. Donna, Carol's assistant at the magazine and her other close friend, had come in to straighten up the apartment.

"Paul's so upset," Mrs Martin confided to Carol and Larry. "He didn't go to school Monday or Tuesday. He went down to Washington Square to sit by the fountain there. Last summer Ronnie and Cindy used to coax him to go down there with them. They said they felt funny hanging around there alone, but with him it was all right. They liked mingling with the college kids that hung out there. It made them feel grown up."

The early April day was unseasonably warm. In Washington Square Park mothers with baby carriages were taking advantage of the weather to sit on the benches. Students huddled around the waterless fountain – absorbed in conversation. A bearded youth, his head thrown back and eyes shut, played a guitar and sang a late sixties song about Vietnam. A few elderly ladies braved the chill to enjoy the sun. A bum – strayed from the Bowery – peed against a tree.

Despite the starkness of the trees and the barren earth, Ronnie felt the scent of spring in the air. She walked with Cindy towards the fountain, their usual destination. So Paul wasn't here with them – they were doing okay.

28

"Ronnie, we've been cutting an awful lot." Cindy was apprehensive. "If my mother finds out, she'll kill me."

"She won't find out. If she does, tell her you had your period and you went shopping in Bergdorf's to forget about the cramps. She always understands that. We'll go to Bergdorf's later," she added as Cindy opened her mouth to point out this gap in the story.

The sweater Ronnie was wearing under her coat had been bought on one such trip. After she'd got it home, Cindy had decided she hated it. Why did Mom get so pissed every time Cindy gave her something like this? So what if the sweater cost over a hundred bucks – Cindy's folks didn't care.

"If my mother ever found out about last week, she'd ship me off to a convent," Cindy predicted. "One where they still wear those Dracula habits."

"It was part of our sociology class." Ronnie dismissed this.

"To fool around with those guys in Spanish Harlem?"

"Your folks don't have to know everything. They just pay the bills."

Why did Daddy have to arrange for her to spend next weekend with him instead of this weekend? She didn't buy that shit about his being into two weekends of therapy. He'd sworn he was through with all that crap. He'd been in analysis for three years. He'd tried encounter groups and TM, nude marathons and mind-expansion groups. *He was spending the weekend with Tiger.*

He'd never kept his women around the apartment when she was there until he started seeing Tiger. When she woke up the last time she'd stayed with Daddy, Tiger had still been hanging around him.

29

"Ronnie, I don't think we ought to be here." Cindy was blinking, the way she always did when she was nervous.

"Cindy, we made a pact." Ronnie's voice was accusing. "We're going to that quack Lisa told us about. We'll get a prescription for the Pill."

"I don't think he's supposed to give it to us." Cindy's blinking accelerated.

"We'll tell him we're eighteen." That's what Lisa had said to do. "He won't care. He just wants the money. The old creep's got a drinking problem."

"What's the name of that training you said your old man is taking?" Cindy demanded out of left field. "I heard somebody on the bus talking about it, I think."

"AMO," Ronnie said shortly. She didn't believe Daddy was taking any training. He wasn't seeing *her* this weekend because he couldn't spare time away from Tiger.

"Amo, amas, amat," Cindy conjugated from first year Latin. "I love, you love, he loves. What is it? A new kind of group grope?"

"They train you how to love yourself," Ronnie told her. "If you have a better image of yourself, then you can cope with problems. That's their *schtick*."

This was the weekend Daddy was supposed to take her to that new club that just opened up. *He had promised.*

Four

On Friday morning Lieutenant Jenkins sat in a leather-upholstered armchair in the large, square, elegantly furnished reception room of the Fairbanks School, just off Fifth Avenue in the Sixties. The school had once been the graystone mansion of a wealthy Manhattan socialite, and from the exterior still bore that same aura. Now, after the clang of a bell, students were charging up and down the highly polished mahogany staircase that circled up to the four floors of classrooms.

In a small office off the reception room a feminine student was crying noisily. She was in consultation with the school psychiatrist, the vivacious young receptionist had informed him.

"There's always somebody in there bawling," she told Jenkins. She lowered her voice but her words carried to him. "Spoiled brats. Most of them need a kick in the ass."

"Or parents who are less permissive," Jenkins suggested. The receptionist's eyes were bright with curiosity. She knew he was here to question the principal about Ronnie.

Sometimes Jenkins complained about the fees at Kathy's parochial school; the tuition here was probably five times as high. But Janet and he had only one child to see through school, and with the turmoil in the city schools – even out in Queens – he wanted to know that Kathy was safe.

But Ronnie Evans, despite attending the exclusive Fairbanks School and circulating with the children of the affluent, had been pushed to her death. He could keep his cool on almost any case but something like this, involving a child, disturbed him. He looked at Kathy each day with a special awareness of how precious she was to him.

Jenkins appraised the students who were moving past the reception room into the adjoining wing of the building. They were dressed in a style abstained by most of their peers – no jeans, no rumpled slacks, no beat-up sneakers here. Nor the unprepossessing parochial school uniform that Kathy had worn since the first grade. The clothes of these kid, he decided, unmistakably bore labels from Saks, Bergdorf's and Bloomingdale's.

"The students are not allowed to wear jeans." The receptionist read his mind. "Slacks have to have a crease, and the boys have to wear ties or turtleneck shirts under their jackets. Isn't that the pits?"

"Don't they rebel?"

"A few." The receptionist giggled. "One girl comes to school every day in beat-up jeans and sneakers and changes in the washroom. But she's showing her rebellion."

A bell buzzed on the desk. The receptionist flipped a switch.

"Yes, sir." She listened for a moment. "I'll send him right in." She gestured towards the door to the principal's office. "His Majesty awaits."

Dr Edmondsen rose from behind the executive desk to greet him.

"Sorry to have kept you waiting, Lieutenant Jenkins," he said perfunctorily. "Please sit down." His eyes were guarded. He was nervous that Ronnie's death might in some way reflect on the school. "We've all been terribly shaken by the tragedy."

"Ronnie had been a student here for five years, I understand." Jenkins knew he would learn nothing from this pompous ass, but he would go through the motions. "How was she regarded by her teachers?"

"Ronnie was a sweet, lovely child. Everybody liked her. Never a troublemaker. Her grades were consistently good, sometimes very high. It's inconceivable that something like this could have happened." Unconsciously he tapped on his desk with one fingernail.

"There was no drug problem, no hostility on the part of another student?"

Edmondsen bristled. "We have no drug problem in the school."

Was there any school without a drug problem? Jenkins asked himself.

"I told you, everybody liked Ronnie. She was one of those students who make a conscientious effort to be well-regarded both by her peers and the faculty."

"Mrs Evans told me that her closest friend here was Cindy Weinberg," Jenkins said. "I'd like to talk to Cindy for a few minutes, if I may."

Edmondsen's face tightened. "Shouldn't this be discussed first with her parents? I don't know that I have the authority . . ."

"I spoke with Mrs Weinberg at home," Jenkins interrupted. "You may check if you like. Cindy is allowed to talk to me without a lawyer in attendance," he explained dryly. "It would be more convenient here than at the family apartment."

He was anxious to talk to Cindy away from her nervous mother. When Corelli had questioned Cindy earlier in the week, Mrs Weinberg had answered the questions before Cindy could get her thoughts together.

"It means she'll have to be called from class." Edmondsen was irritated. However, he buzzed the receptionist.

The receptionist showed Jenkins to a small room across the hall. He settled himself in the chair behind the desk. Cindy would be sent to him in a few moments. Jenkins stirred restlessly as he waited. The atmosphere of the Fairbanks school was a turn-off for him. The sheltered little world that Jason Evans had bought for his daughter had not saved her from murder.

The door opened slowly. Cindy came into the room. She was wearing a long black skirt, almost to the ankle, the slit at the side decorous because of the school's dress code. Janet had bought Kathy one like it for her birthday last month. He'd flinched when Janet told him the price. Times like that he felt relieved that they had only one child.

"Cindy, I want to ask you a few questions." His voice was gentle. He remembered how hard Cindy had taken Ronnie's death.

"Okay." She lifted her head with an air of faint defiance. Had her mother called the school after he got off the phone and warned her about what she could say?

"Cindy, did you see Ronnie during last weekend?"

"No. She spent the weekend with her father." Cindy was fighting tears.

"When was the last time you saw her?" Don't let her bawl, Jenkins prayed. He had to have some answers.

"After school on Friday. We went to the Mid-Manhattan Library together. We both had to get a report in on Monday. If we didn't, we could flunk. Ronnie was going to do the report at her father's apartment." Cindy's voice broke.

"I want you to think carefully now," he leaned forward, his eyes compassionate. "Was there anyone who was angry at Ronnie? It might have been somebody who seemed completely normal, but was sick inside. Cindy, who hated Ronnie?"

"Nobody!" Cindy insisted. "Everybody liked Ronnie. She was one of those kids who never fought with anybody. You know, sweet and wanting to help."

"What about boys? Ronnie was a very pretty girl. Did she have a special boyfriend?" *Some creep who pushed her off the terrace?*

"Ronnie didn't bother with guys. I mean, she liked them and all, but she didn't chase after them the way some of the girls at school do. She was kind of shy." Cindy dropped her eyes to her hands.

"Paul Martin was a special friend, wasn't he?"

Cindy lifted her head. She seemed startled. "Oh sure, but Paul wasn't a boyfriend. I mean, they lived in the same building, and they kind of grew up together, that's all." Cindy hesitated. "When Paul was at school here, everybody thought he was gay." Jenkins started. He was old-fashioned, he chastised himself. These kids knew — and discussed — everything. "Ronnie never believed that. She never believed bad of anybody."

"Somebody killed her," Jenkins reminded. "We have to find out who did it."

35

"I wouldn't know anything about that." Cindy's eyes were guarded as they met his, but he spied indecisiveness there for an infinitesimal fragment of time. *Cindy knew something.* Somebody – probably her mother – had warned her not to talk. Not to become involved. Because then Cindy's life would be in danger?

"Cindy, I want you to search your mind," Jenkins urged. Damn, this kid could help them. "Wasn't there one person who disliked Ronnie? Someone who might not have a real reason, but in a mixed-up way felt that Ronnie had done something objectionable? This is terribly important." He waited, frustration building in him because he sensed Cindy's alarm.

"I don't know anything about that, but her father might." Her eyes were guileless as they met his. "Why don't you ask Mr Evans?" She was scared to talk, but she was trying to push him in the right direction. Somebody Jason Evans knew had a reason to kill Ronnie. That was whom Cindy Weinberg suspected.

Four hours later Jenkins sat back in a brown suede-upholstered armchair placed before a glass-topped Mies van der Rohe table that served as Jason Evans's desk. He gazed out upon a view of Manhattan that extended to the bridges that laced the Bronx. Jason was chewing out a vocalist who wanted to remain in Acapulco a week beyond an imminent recording session.

"Look, Gina, don't give me any more of that shit," he wound up brusquely. "You be here on schedule or you won't record for anybody else in this town! I promise you that." His eyes glinted dangerously as he slammed down the phone.

Rotten temper, Jenkins thought. Was it bad enough to have provoked him into pushing Ronnie off the terrace? He had taken an instant dislike to Jason Evans. Maybe that was why his mind toyed at intervals with considering Evans as the murderer. Realistically he acknowledged that there wasn't a shred of evidence to lead to such a conclusion. Not even a gut reaction.

"I'm sorry to bother you again, Mr Evans," he apologized. "But we can't afford to leave any loopholes open. I'd like to go over again exactly what happened that Sunday. The whole day," he emphasized.

Jenkins sat forward, listening while Jason repeated his initial spiel.

"I took her home early because she had a school report to do," he wound up. "You know kids. She left it to the last minute. I dropped her off at a few minutes past three. Her mother had told her she was going to the country with her friend Iris." Jason was sarcastic. He knew Carol had been with Larry Ransome.

"Did you hear from her any time during the afternoon?" It was easier than asking, where the hell were you when Ronnie was pushed from the terrace.

"No." Jason's face tensed. "I never saw her again."

"She didn't phone you to say she'd finished the report?" Jenkins pursued.

Suddenly Jason's eyes were hostile. "She couldn't have reached me." Evans knew what he was after. "I was in my recording studio with Tiger Rhodes, working on a new release. At times like that I always take the phone off the hook." Okay, he had an alibi.

"Was Ronnie in good spirits over the weekend?"

"Great spirits. We spent the weekend at Southampton,

walked a lot on the beach. We slept late Sunday. All that fresh air, I suppose. After we'd had breakfast, we listened to some tapes. That's when Ronnie admitted she had a report to do. She figured she'd better go home and do it. It was hard for her to study at my place." He smiled wryly. "Too many distractions. She loved messing around with the recording equipment. Sometimes I'd tape her singing along with one of my groups. She got a great charge out of that."

"Mr Evans, I'm going to ask you something I've asked before," Jenkins acknowledged, "but with your mind clear now you may come up with information we can use. Who among your artists – or would-be artists – might have harbored a grudge?"

"Any singer or musician I've turned down in the past twelve years," Evans said without emotion. He didn't want his production company involved with Ronnie's murder. "Would you want a list of everybody I've aud- itioned and rejected?"

"I doubt that Homicide has the facilities to follow through on that," Jenkins conceded. "But wasn't there one person – or a few – who made threats, created disturbances?"

Jason shook his head, leaned forward, his jaw clenched. "I want that bastard caught. I want to be there in the front row in the courtroom when he's tried. I wish I could see him fry. I'm glad we have capital punishment in this state!" His eyes narrowed with hate, then clouded over. "Look, I never asked. I couldn't bring myself to ask . . ." He paused. "Was Ronnie molested before she was thrown off the terrace?"

"She wasn't touched." Jenkins was astonished by his

own gentleness. He detested Jason Evans, but he understood a father's concern that his daughter might have been raped before she was killed. "The autopsy confirmed that."

Jenkins left Evans's office and returned to his own. Corelli was waiting for him. He'd been doing a check on Jason Evans.

"He probably has enough enemies to over-populate Riker's Island." Corelli leaned back in his chair and rested his feet on the pulled-out lower desk drawer. "His casting couch has to be re-covered twice a year. It's possible some vengeful broad got back at him by killing his daughter."

Jenkins shook his head. "I've got a gut reaction that says no to that."

"This is a murder with a motive. That's my gut reaction," Corelli retaliated. "This creep had a motive," he reiterated. "A sick motive, but a motive. The girl knew him – "

"Or her," Jenkins intervened.

Corelli grinned. "For the sake of simplicity, let's use 'he'. He was inside the apartment. No evidence of forced entry. Ronnie Evans was a bright, city-bred youngster – she knew not to let a stranger in. Two locks, television security surveillance in the lobby, and a doorman to call up and announce people. Whoever pushed her knew her."

Jenkins sighed and shoved back his chair. "Let's go over to Cosmos for coffee and a Danish."

Shortly after three-thirty Jenkins presented himself at the door to the Martins' apartment. He had told the doorman to announce him, but he had not waited for an invitation. As he emerged from the elevator, he spied an open door to the right. Mrs Martin was waiting to receive him.

"The doorman said you were coming up." Her annoyance was obvious. "I don't know what else we can tell you."

"I just have a few more questions," he soothed. "To make sure our report is accurate."

"Come in, Lieutenant." She was straining to be polite. "I have to leave for an appointment soon."

A huge Bernese pup, whose paws indicated he would be even huger in six months, galloped towards him. "Machiavelli, down." Mrs Martin reached for the pup's collar before he could jump up and greet Jenkins in the manner he considered hospitable.

"Hi there, Machiavelli." Jenkins bestowed a friendly pat. Kathy would be wild about this character. He ought to be out in the country with ten acres of fields to run through.

"I'll put him in Paul's room." Mrs. Martin excused herself.

She returned in a few moments and sat down in a chair across from Jenkins.

"Paul is just beginning to accept Ronnie's death." Her eyes were troubled. "Your coming here again will bring it all back." Her eyes strayed to a sunburst wall clock. She didn't realize he had planned his arrival to coincide with Paul's coming home from school. "Are you going to question him again?"

"Very briefly." Jenkins had sensed it would unnerve Paul to question him at school. "Now if you'll just confirm a few statements you made earlier . . ." He whipped out his notebook.

40

He had just finished the perfunctory interview with Mrs Martin when the doorbell rang. He wouldn't have to drag this out any longer, he thought with relief. In another room Machiavelli began to bark frenziedly.

"That's Paul." Mrs Martin rose to her feet and hurried to the door. Jenkins heard her explain to Paul that he was in the apartment. He remembered what Cindy had said about the gay label. Kids could be as cruel as the Mafia. Paul's lean, aesthetic face, his dark curling hair, his sensitivity, made him vulnerable.

"Hello, Paul." Jenkins's smile was meant to be reassuring.

"Machiavelli expects me to take him out now," Paul said, his eyes accusing.

"He's too much for me to handle," Mrs Martin explained. "Paul, Lieutenant Jenkins won't keep you long. Then you can walk Machiavelli."

To the background of Machiavelli's vociferous barking Jenkins questioned Paul. The kid was upset, he realized. His eyes kept wandering around the room. He massaged one hand with the other. He was afraid of displeasing his mother, Jenkins surmised. What were they trying to hide?

"Paul, think carefully. Wasn't there someone who hated Ronnie? Hated her enough to push her off the terrace?"

"No!" All at once Paul was shouting. "It was crazy. She shouldn't have died! She didn't do anything bad!"

The defiant, defensive glow in Paul's eyes triggered Jenkins's curiosity. He wasn't going to find out anything from Paul Martin. But he was damn sure that the kid – like Cindy Weinberg – knew more than he was letting on.

41

Waiting for the down elevator Jenkins made a snap decision. He left the bank of elevators and walked down to the twelfth floor. He hesitated a moment then decided to ring the doorbell at the right of the Evans apartment. The name-plate read 'Roberts'.

"Who is it?" a fluttery feminine voice demanded.

Mrs. Roberts was nervous because he had not been buzzed up. The doorman had said all the tenants were nervous since the murder. With tears welling in his eyes the doorman had talked about Ronnie: "I can't believe that sweet young girl is dead. Do you know, one day about a week before it happened she brought me back a shake from Baskin & Robbins when she went there for ice-cream? How many kids would do something nice like that?"

"This is Detective Jenkins of Homicide, Mrs Roberts," he announced himself. He pulled out his badge and held it up before the peephole.

The door opened. A small, heavy blonde in her early fifties, clad in a concealing hostess gown, pulled it wide. She gazed up at him with guarded politeness. "Yes?"

"I'm investigating Ronnie Evans's murder," Jenkins said. "I'd like to ask you some questions."

"Of course." She gestured him inside. There'd be no trouble persuading this lady to talk, though he doubted she would have much to contribute. Still, one tiny thread could be important.

"I came home from visiting my son just two hours after it happened," she volunteered. "It's terrifying to know that something like that could happen in a building with such fine security. I jump at any little sound I hear in the night now."

"Mrs Roberts, how long have you lived in this apartment?"

"Oh, I'm one of the original tenants." She hesitated, seeming to prod herself to speak. "I know everybody thought she was so sweet sugar wouldn't melt in her mouth, but they didn't hear what I've heard in the years we've been neighbors. I don't know if I should say this . . ." All at once she was flustered by her candor.

"Please go on," Jenkins urged.

"Ronnie was a case. She had an awful temper – and the language that could come from that pretty mouth." She flinched in recall. "Her mother ought to have horse-whipped her for what she put her through. Not just the terrible language and the way she reviled Carol. Ronnie physically misused her mother. I've seen the scratches on her mother's arms, the bruises on her face. Carol took it all, dragging Ronnie from one analyst to another. The worst time, though, was about a year and a half ago. Carol started to see a very nice man." She hesitated. "She's still seeing him – but she tries to keep it from Ronnie. Ronnie was jealous. Carol came home from the theater one night and the minute she walked in, Ronnie started screaming about terrible pains in her stomach. She told Carol she had taken a handful of Xanax. Carol called for an ambulance and then phoned Eleanor – a neighbor who's a nurse – to come down. I was so shaken. I wanted to go in and offer to help, but I wouldn't know what to do . . ."

"What happened?" Jenkins prodded.

"Ronnie kept on wailing until Eleanor said they had to try to make her throw up the pills. When Eleanor tried to shove a finger down her throat, Ronnie bit her then admitted it was a hoax. She was punishing her mother for going out to the theater." Mrs. Roberts sighed. "And even then Carol stopped Eleanor from yelling at Ronnie for frightening them to death like that."

Jenkins left the apartment house and headed east, his mind replaying the interview with Mrs Roberts. With a temper like that Ronnie Evans must have made enemies. A temper she had inherited from her father.

At the corner Jenkins stopped for a light. A man stood there selling red roses from a corrugated carton. He pulled out his wallet, bought a bunch. Kathy was mad for red roses. What would he do if somebody pushed Kathy out a window? Not that it would be such a tragedy, considering they lived in the lower-floor apartment of a two-family house in Queens.

Five

Carol sat jackknifed in a tense, tight ball at one end of the sofa. The living room was in semi-darkness because the wall of drapes remained drawn to conceal the view of the terrace. She was agonizingly conscious that it was one week ago – plus minutes – that she had glanced up from the car to see Ronnie plummeting to her death. She had not gone back to the office since. Max understood that she couldn't come back yet. Tears filled her eyes as she remembered the beautiful white roses Max had sent.

She told herself, over and over again, that she must learn to deal with her grief. Yet, except for going to Ronnie's funeral, she had not left the apartment since that awful day. She allowed the answering machine to pick up all her phone calls. Other than Larry, she saw only Iris and Donna who visited for a little while each evening, each trying to divert her from the self-incrimination that absorbed her. *My fault Ronnie's dead. I should have been here when she came home. I should have allowed her to have a dog.*

Larry stayed with her every hour he could spare away from his office. He prepared breakfast, made sure lunch-makings were in the refrigerator, and scolded her when he realized they were untouched. Each evening he brought home dinner from Cosmos or take-out Chinese. They slept on the opened-up convertible sofa because she couldn't bear to go into the bedroom. Each night he held her in his arms – knowing this was not the time to make love.

She started at the sound of a key in the door. Larry was back from a drive to Westchester County with a client. The door swung open. He walked in – his smile meant to be reassuring.

"I got adventurous for dinner." He crossed to kiss her tenderly, headed for the kitchen. "I picked up a roast chicken and a salad at the Associated. And a pint of Ben & Jerry's for dessert." He put the frozen yogurt in the freezer compartment, checked below. "Carol, you didn't have lunch."

"I wasn't hungry."

"Hey, that won't do," he chided, his eyes somber. "But let's have the chicken while it's still hot." He went into the kitchenette for plates and flatware.

What am I going to do about Larry? I know what he's thinking. But I can't marry him now. Can't he see that? It would be as though Ronnie's death had paved the way for us. I know we can't go on this way – but how will I survive without him?

"Carol, come and get it," he ordered lightly, bringing the food to the table.

In the aura of unreality that was her constant companion, Carol left the sofa to join Larry in the dining area. She would eat because he insisted.

"I've been thinking," he began when he'd cleared away the dishes and brought out the Ben & Jerry's and a pair of fanciful ice-cream plates. She shivered – Ronnie had adored those plates. "Perhaps you ought to move from here." He meant, *move in with me.*

46

"I can't." Carol flinched at the prospect. This was where she had lived with Ronnie for almost five years. To leave would be an admission that Ronnie was gone. "I can't do anything until that fiend is caught." *Will I feel any differently then?*

"Carol, it could be a year." Larry walked over to flip on the air-conditioner, removing his jacket en route. "It could be two years."

"Why aren't the police coming up with something?" she demanded with sudden hostility. "It's as though nothing happened."

"They're searching for some thread to follow. They're still questioning people in the building."

"A stranger couldn't get in past the doorman." How many times had she said that? "You know what tight security we have here!" But why would anyone here have wanted to kill Ronnie? How had he – or she – got into the apartment? Ronnie was killed by somebody they knew. Even the cops thought so, even though they hadn't come out and said that.

"The doorman could have stepped away from the lobby to flag down a cab. It only takes a minute for somebody to slip inside." Larry tried to sound matter of fact. "Carol, you have to go back to the office tomorrow morning. They need you. Work's piling up."

"Not yet," she resisted. "I can't face people. I can't face their compassion."

Larry understood what she meant. He had been through the trauma of losing his wife and son.

Carol found it difficult to talk even with Iris and Donna, her two closest friends in New York. Only with Paul could she communicate. He was so stricken – mirroring her own desolation. He had come down each day after school this week to water the flower boxes on the terrace. She would never set foot out there again. Paul had done whatever was necessary out there. His grief almost matched her own.

She had asked Paul not to bring down his over-sized, awkward pup. Ronnie had adored Machiavelli. She had pleaded to be allowed to buy one of the pups from the same litter. Why hadn't she allowed Ronnie to have the puppy? Carol agonized. A puppy would have rushed to protect her.

"You can't be a recluse, Carol. You've got to move back into life."

"I need time," she hedged.

"We'll talk about it later," Larry relented. "And when we've finished eating, I'll run to my apartment for some more clothes. I'm running out of things." He hesitated. "You want me to stay for a while longer?"

"Larry, yes!" How could she bear to be here alone, with memories of Ronnie lurking in every shadow? But she could not say to him, *Larry, move in completely*. That would be acknowledging that Ronnie was forever gone.

They were finishing up their coffee when the doorbell rang. Carol started. It couldn't be detectives on a Sunday evening. She was ambivalent about their presence. She wanted to know that they were working to find the monster who had murdered Ronnie, yet each time a detective came into the apartment, she was assaulted by a recall of those horrible moments in front of the apartment house.

Larry went to the door and pulled it wide.

"Hi, Iris."

"I was going out tonight but I got stood up," she

said cheerfully. "I figured I'd come down here and nag you two."

"I have to go over to my place for some things," Larry said, grateful for her presence. "Have a cup of coffee with Carol and tell her about your latest novel." Iris always had a fresh supply of humorous anecdotes about what she called 'my erotic hystericals'.

"You go on, Larry. I'll pour myself coffee. I know my way around here." She turned to Carol. "More coffee for you?"

"I've been drinking so much coffee I need oars to get about. But yes, more coffee." She was glad not to be alone while Larry was gone.

Larry left. Iris poured two mugs of coffee and brought them into the living room.

"In a way I'm glad this creep stood me up," Iris confided. "I don't feel comfortable going out with a guy fifteen years younger than me. It's almost incestuous."

"You're a damned attractive woman. Don't forever look at the calendar." Carol forced herself into small talk.

"I'm a forty-nine-year-old woman who got dumped overboard four years ago." That was when she had moved into the building, Carol recalled. They'd met on a rainy Sunday evening in the laundry room and clicked immediately. "I never talked to you about the divorce, did I?"

"No." She'd sensed right off that this was a subject off-limits, and respected this. Usually they talked about Iris's two college student sons – who surfaced at intervals – or about her post-divorce career.

"Hank was having a middle-age crisis. I was too busy

editing confession stories to realize it. With him it was a big production. Suddenly he was chasing after women half his age. One figured he was a great meal ticket. She went after a permanent deal – and won."

"How's the new book coming along?" Larry was right. She had to get back on the treadmill again. How long could she live on Xanax and sympathy?

Carol leaned back, listened to Iris's colorful report of her latest 'erotic hysterical', grateful for her presence. After twenty-five years of marriage Iris had had to rebuild a whole new life for herself. *She* had built her life around Ronnie. But in these last eighteen months Larry had brought something new and precious into her life. *I didn't cheat Ronnie because of Larry. I know I didn't.*

The phone was raucous in its intrusion. For an instant Carol didn't move. These last days she had become accustomed to Larry's picking up the phone, shielding her. Iris smiled, eyebrows lifted questioningly. Carol forced herself to reach for the phone.

"Hello."

"Jason." He identified himself tersely, as though it were necessary. Phone voices, she thought, live forever in your memory.

"What do you want?" She was in no mood for his abrasiveness. She didn't need to cater to him anymore.

"I've hired a private investigator," he told her. "He'll want to talk to you."

"The police are investigating. They've been in and out of here every day. Let him talk to them." Perversely she was irritated that Jason had taken this step, which she had vowed to do herself. Yet Jason could afford a two-hundred-dollar-a-day private investigator. She couldn't.

"The cops have got a dozen cases to follow up," Jason said impatiently. "The guy's name is Henderson. He'll call you tomorrow."

She made an instantaneous decision. "I'll be at the office." *Why do I always feel defensive with Jason? Even now.* "I have to earn a living."

"He'll call you at the office at ten tomorrow," Jason amended. "Damn it, don't you want to know who killed Ronnie? If you'd been home when you were supposed to be, it wouldn't have happened!"

"It's fourteen years too late for you to start being a father!" Shaken by the accusation that haunted her unceasingly, Carol slammed down the phone.

"Jason's hired some private detective," she told Iris, her voice uneven. "I'm supposed to cooperate." It was as though, even in death, Jason was trying to wrest Ronnie from her.

"He's got another record on the charts." Iris shrugged. "He can afford it."

Jason had always made a point of keeping Ronnie out of his publicity. Nobody was supposed to know he had a daughter as old as Ronnie. His biography lied about his age. Occasionally he'd talk about 'my little girl', inferring that she was fresh out of diapers. He had a compulsion to be seen in all the 'in' places with girls twenty years younger than he was.

The intercom buzzed. Carol frowned. The doormen all knew Larry was staying here, that he had a key. She left the sofa and crossed to the dining area, pushed the talk button.

"Yes?"

"Detective Jenkins is here. He'd like to know if he can come up for a few minutes."

Carol sighed. Even on a Sunday evening? But Jenkins was the detective with the fourteen-year-old daughter.

"Ask him to come up, please." She walked back to the sofa. "It's one of the detectives."

"I'll split." Iris rose to her feet.

"Stay," Carol urged. "He'll only be here a few minutes. I can't imagine what else he wants to ask." *When are they going to leave me alone? There's nothing else I can tell them.*

The doorbell rang. Iris went to admit Lieutenant Jenkins. Her face strained, Carol rose to her feet.

"I'm sorry to bother you, Mrs Evans," he apologized, "but I keep thinking we're missing something."

"What do you want me to tell you, Lieutenant?" *What else can I tell him? That I can't sleep for blaming myself for not being here when she needed me? That I feel as much her killer as the person who pushed her off the terrace?*

"I'd like to go through Ronnie's room again. More fully this time," he said guardedly. "Maybe there's a note stuffed in a jacket pocket, a piece of paper somewhere with a name on it."

"Do you have to do that?" Carol demanded, recoiling from the prospect of a stranger going through Ronnie's personal belongings. Later, much later, she would have to do something about Ronnie's clothes. *But I can't think about that now.*

"Mrs Evans, I know it's no consolation, but I can understand how you feel," Lieutenant Jenkins told her.

"We want to find Ronnie's killer. I don't sleep nights thinking about it. I look at my kid, and I tell myself I can't waste a minute."

"Do you think he's going to come back and try to kill me, too?" Carol asked. At intervals she considered this. Even with the apartment door locks changed.

"I don't think so, but we don't honestly know what he'll do until we have him in custody," he conceded. "We want to nail him, Mrs Evans." He hesitated. "Is it all right if I go into Ronnie's bedroom?"

Carol took a deep breath, closed her eyes for a moment. Lieutenant Jenkins didn't have to ask her permission. This was part of his job.

"Go ahead, Lieutenant," she forced herself to say.

She couldn't bring herself to look into Ronnie's room, yet at the same time she yearned to walk in there and feel Ronnie's presence. Ronnie had been so proud of her room. She had loved her stereo system. The ultra-feminine dressing table, laden with the incredible array of nail polish and eye-shadows given to her by Iris during Iris's brief beauty editor period, before she was selling regularly in the paperback field. Cindy and Ronnie would spend hours in there, trying out eye-shadows and way-out shades of nail polish.

Lieutenant Jenkins had left the bedroom door open. Carol's eyes were drawn compulsively in its direction. Ronnie's huge stuffed panda – as large as a three-year-old child and given to her by Jason three years ago – no longer sat on the bed with the other stuffed animals. She had felt an odd twinge when Ronnie had taken it with her to Jason's apartment several weekends ago and left it there. It was as though Ronnie was emotionally removing herself to Jason's apartment. Was the panda sitting on the bed in Jason's guest room now? Had Ronnie slept with it when she spent that last weekend at Jason's apartment?

She shivered, despite the warmth of the room. Trying to visualize Ronnie in Jason's luxurious apartment . . .

Six

Emerging from the bathroom, her tall lissome body semi-concealed by a sheer black nightie, Ronnie went to sit at the edge of the turned-down bed. She reached to pull the over-sized stuffed panda into her arms. Her eyes were stormy, her mouth set in rage. Why did she have to take the AMO training this weekend? Because it would take her out of Daddy's way?

Tiger wasn't here tonight, but Daddy would spend all day tomorrow – until she came home from the training – with that whore. Daddy said the training session might go on till two in the morning. She was to call him from the hotel where the sessions were held and he'd come and get her.

"Ronnie?" Jason called tentatively from the other side of the door. "You in bed?"

"Yes," she sulked, sliding beneath the sheets and pulling the panda in beside her. She thrust the pillows behind her, rested against the headboard.

Jason came in and sat at the edge of the bed.

"Baby, you're angry with me," he reproached. "I'm telling you, you'll be glad you've taken the training. You couldn't take it if I hadn't first," he said with pride. "That's one of AMO's regulations."

"Mom won't like it." Her voice was defiant.

"We're not telling her," he reminded her, his smile smug. "Our secret, baby."

"Why did we have to come home so early?" They had been having such fun at that club. Everybody thought she was sensational. Daddy had told them she was a new young singer he was preparing to record. Why did she have to sing flat like Mom? She loved music.

"Honey, you have to be up early and over at that hotel ballroom. It's just for two weekends. You're going to feel so marvelous afterwards. I'm a new man."

"I like the old one," Ronnie shot back.

"Don't be mad at me," he chided, lowered his mouth to kiss her good-night.

Deliberately Ronnie moved so that his mouth collided with hers. Her arms tightened about his neck. But all at once he was pulling away from her.

"Hey, that was quite a good-night kiss," he said unsteadily.

Ronnie wondered if Tiger was already there, hiding out in the living room. *I hate that slut!*

"Sleep well, baby. I'll wake you at seven."

She tried to stay awake, listening for sounds from the other room – but tiredness overtook her. She slept until she felt Jason gently shaking her by the shoulder.

"Rise and shine, baby. I'll have breakfast waiting for you."

She dressed quickly in her Calvin Klein jeans and a t-shirt with the message 'Happiness Is Here'. Daddy had said it would be a great outfit to wear to AMO. She stared hard at her reflection in the mirror. This morning, with no make-up on, she looked about twelve. Daddy said they mixed the teenagers in with the grown-ups. Two hundred people in one ballroom – all with their neuroses hanging out. It was enough to make anybody puke.

In a fit of irritation she reached for her make-up kit and went the full route, then left the bedroom and moved into the living room. The door to the den was wide open. Her gaze moved down the hall. The guest-room door was open, too. Daddy wanted her to think Tiger wasn't here. But she could smell the heavy scent of that weird perfume Tiger wore. She must be holed up in the studio, waiting for *her* to split. She must have been here all night.

"Come on. Sit down and eat hearty," Jason ordered. "You won't get a meal break until sometime in the afternoon – depending on how the session's going."

"What about pee breaks?"

"You won't have to pee in your pants," he promised cheerfully. "They let you out in sections."

Ronnie ate, smoldering inside because she knew Tiger was probably conked out on the chaise in the studio. Why didn't Daddy send *her* to AMO? Nothing had gone right since he met her.

Ronnie felt uneasy approaching the AMO experience. Daddy got a charge out of way-out situations. Why couldn't he come with her? But he said that wasn't allowed. It was something she had to do by herself.

They left the apartment. He drove her in the red Jaguar to the hotel where she was to begin her fifty-hour-plus training. At the entrance to the ballroom he kissed her on one cheek, grinned in reassurance, swatted her on the rump and watched her go inside.

Ronnie signed in, picked up her button with her name on it and pinned it on her t-shirt. She allowed a volunteer to show her to a seat. She wore the limpid baby stare that invariably convinced everybody she was an adorable, wistful innocent, but covertly her eyes tabulated her neighbors.

The door was closed. She fought down a sense of panic. The one hundred and ninety-nine other people here for the training appeared to be as tense as she was. You could smell the tension, she thought with distaste. All the drapes were drawn tight, obliterating a sense of time. The exit signs had a big, black NO! painted over the traditional sign.

They'd be here for at least twelve-and-a-half hours. It was supposed to be a fifty-hour training program split into four sessions, but Daddy had admitted that everybody forgot the time. He'd stayed in this room from nine one morning until two the next morning, with only one pee break and one meal break.

Somebody was moving among the trainees, collecting watches. No timepieces were allowed. No gum. No cigarettes. A volunteer stood up to explain, in an irritatingly monotonous voice, the ground rules for the training. Then the trainer mounted the dais. A pompous ass, Ronnie thought. Why was he staring at them all like they were garbage?

"You're all a bunch of jerks!" he spat at them, bringing words to his expression. "You're here because you're so screwed-up you don't know where to turn next."

Daddy must have flipped out. Who had to pay all that money to be called a jerk? She'd stay here today because she didn't have the guts to get up and walk out. *Nobody was walking out.* But she wouldn't come back tomorrow, no matter what Daddy said. What did the money mean to him? He spent that in one night around town.

She shifted in her straight-backed hard chair. The seats were packed together like at an over-subscribed school benefit. Her butt was falling asleep. This whole scene was screwy. But gradually she found herself drawn to those in the training who asked for the microphone so that they might speak. What assholes they were to turn their guts inside out that way!

A tall, florid-faced man of about fifty, in an Yves Saint-Laurent shirt and slacks, was declaiming with an intensity that demanded the other trainees' attention.

"Look at me. I'm fifty years old. I head a talent agency that controls half the personalities on TV. I can make or break the careers of some of the biggest names on the networks. I'm a VIP and I feel like shit. I've just gone through my third divorce." On and on he raved, about his sexual dysfunction and the frustration this caused him.

What was Daddy doing right now? Ronnie kept her gaze fixed on the talent agent, but her mind was weaving fantasies about Daddy and that Tiger whore. She'd sneak into the studio when Daddy and Tiger were sleeping and she'd shave off every inch of that bottle-blonde hair. She'd puncture those silicone boobs and watch them go flat like a pair of dead balloons.

What the hell was going on now? Ronnie's eyes widened in shock. People were handing in candy bars, sandwiches, cookies – the caches they'd stashed away to consume in the privacy of their pee breaks.

The leader was verbally flagellating them again. He wouldn't be satisfied till he'd made them all feel as big as the water-bug she spied crossing across the floor. She wasn't the only one watching the water-bug. This was boring. When would they start getting their pee breaks? She hadn't handed in the Almond Joy stuck away in her jeans pocket.

She could hear stomachs beginning to rumble. The guy next to her was squirming in his seat. Did these creepy trainers expect to keep them sitting here all day? They were a bunch of sadists.

Seven

C arol sat in the living room chair that allowed no view into the bedroom. She clutched a mug of coffee in one hand and focused on Iris, who was trying to divert her from Lieutenant Jenkins's activities in the bedroom. Why couldn't Jenkins have closed the door?

"My agent tells me I'm off the wall to think about trying to switch from erotic hystericals to suspense when I'm making a decent income," Iris sighed dramatically. "But I feel so boxed in."

"Give suspense a whirl," Carol encouraged. "You owe it to yourself." But her thoughts were monopolized by Jenkins' presence in the bedroom. It made her sick to know that a strange man was pawing through Ronnie's clothes. Without seeing she knew he was searching the pockets of every pair of jeans and slacks that hung in Ronnie's closet, the pockets of every jacket and coat.

Carol started at the sound of a key in a lock. Larry was back. She found comfort in his presence.

"Lieutenant Jenkins is here," Carol told him as he walked into the foyer. "He's searching through Ronnie's clothes . . ." Her voice broke.

Before Larry could comment, the detective came striding into the living room. He held a scrap of paper in one hand.

"Mrs Evans, do these names mean anything to you?" He extended the paper. "And this Latin scribble across the bottom – 'Amo, amas, amat'."

"Ronnie took Latin last year . . ." Carol frowned at the names written in Ronnie's tight, small handwriting. Charlie. Amelia. Douglas. Tony. "I don't recognize any of these names. They may be kids at school . . ."

"Who were her particular friends?" Jenkins pushed.

"I've told you," Carol frowned. *We've covered this ground a dozen times*, she thought. "Cindy Weinberg was her best friend at school. She was close with Paul Martin, who lives upstairs. You've questioned both of them."

"I just keep feeling we're walking right past something obvious," Jenkins said with exasperation. "I want to do more checking." Abruptly he returned to the bedroom. This time he pulled the door shut behind him. He was a compassionate, conscientious man, Carol told herself. She ought not to be hostile towards him.

"We're in for a storm," Larry said as thunder rumbled. Carol flinched. Up until two years ago Ronnie had been terrified of thunderstorms. Big as she was, she would crawl into Carol's lap like a two-year-old and cling to her until the last clap of thunder, the last burst of lightning, had dissipated.

"Mrs Evans!" Jenkins's voice snapped them to attention as he pulled the door wide. "What do you know about this?" He was tugging at the drawstrings of the much beat-up duffle bag that Ronnie, in earlier years, had used for her weekend trips to Jason's apartment. More lately she had used it to hold a beach roll. But it wasn't holding a beach roll now.

"Good Lord!" Larry, Carol and Iris gaped at the avalanche of rubber-banded, twenty-dollar bills that cascaded onto the large, square coffee table.

"Where did you find that?" Carol's voice was shrill with disbelief.

"In the right-hand corner of the bedroom closet." Jenkins focused on Carol with accusatory intensity. "What do you know about this?"

"Nothing. It's unbelievable." Her eyes were riveted to the twenty-dollar bills, divided into neat rolls.

"All this money was in your bedroom closet and you know nothing about it?"

"I . . . I never went into Ronnie's bedroom," Carol stammered. "She had a thing about privacy. Her psychiatrist told me to honor that. Her bedroom was her private turf. I have a cleaning woman who comes in one morning a week. She takes care of Ronnie's room." Instinctively Carol turned to Larry. "Where could Ronnie have come up with that kind of money?"

"I suggest we call her father." Larry was grim. "This could be some kind of laundering deal." He rose to his feet – his eyes questioning.

"Please call him," Jenkins concurred.

"Jason's phone numbers are in the book by the phone," Carol told Larry – her mind in turmoil. "I can't remember offhand . . ." *Jenkins suspects me of hiding that money in Ronnie's bedroom.*

"I've never seen so much cash in one place." Iris seemed mesmerized by the notes. She turned to the detective. "How much is there?"

"I'd say somewhere between a hundred and fifty and two hundred thousand dollars. Mrs Evans, we'll have to hold it for evidence." His voice was oddly speculative.

"Of course. I can't imagine how it got into Ronnie's room." All at once Carol was conscious of the ominous, ugly tension in the living room. Iris was remembering how she had objected to Jenkins going into Ronnie's room. He remembered. But she hadn't known about the money!

Larry was on the phone, waiting for Jason. He'd told the person who picked up that it was an urgent matter regarding Ronnie's death. Finally Jason came on the line. "Lieutenant Jenkins wants you here at Carol's apartment," Larry told him. "There's a new development in Ronnie's murder." He paused. "I'll tell him you'll be here in fifteen minutes."

"Do you suppose that whoever . . . whoever killed Ronnie came here looking for that?" Carol asked Jenkins – her mind searching for answers. "He couldn't find it and became furious. He pushed her over the railing." *Oh God, will I ever wash those awful moments from my mind?*

"I don't buy that," Jenkins dismissed. "He could have found it easily enough." The detective checked his watch, turned to Larry. "You're sure Evans is coming over?"

"Reluctantly, but he's coming."

"Whoever killed Ronnie must have known her." It was Jenkins's first outright admission of this. "She was a city kid. She wouldn't have opened the door for a stranger. There was no sign of any tampering with the locks." Methodically Jenkins was repeating the facts, hoping, Carol surmised, to stumble onto some tiny link they had overlooked thus far.

In less than fifteen minutes Jason arrived. He was furious when Jenkins hinted that he had been using Ronnie to hide hot money.

"What the hell's the matter with you?" A vein was distended in Jason's forehead. "You trying to louse me up with the IRS?"

"We're trying to discover why Ronnie had two hundred thousand in twenty-dollar bills concealed in a duffel bag in her bedroom," Jenkins said coldly.

"Ask her mother!" Jason shot back. "What hellish scheme is she into?"

Everyone was startled by the imperious ring of the doorbell. The doorman had not called up, Carol noted. This would be Jenkins's partner, arriving in answer to his summons.

Corelli walked into the apartment with his customary air of faint apology at having to hassle Carol. He talked briefly with Jenkins about the money, then began some low-key questioning. Carol leaned back in her chair – emotionally drained. Jason *had* to have something to do with the money.

She should have taken Ronnie and left the state after the divorce, despite the visitation agreement. She should have run so far away Jason would never have caught up with them. He'd demanded the alternate weekend arrangement – which he had often ignored in the earlier years – only because he knew it infuriated her.

"Mr Evans, do you know of anybody angry enough at you to try to get at you by killing your daughter?" Corelli asked.

"Christ, no! I have the usual amount of enemies for somebody in my position. I've had to tell a lot of people I have no interest in recording them. But that's not a reason for murder."

"To a psychotic it could be," Jenkins picked up. "Or if either of you," his eyes included Carol now, "was ever involved, no matter how casually, in some off-beat cult. One of the cult members could go off the wall and murder-"

"No cults," Jason dismissed brusquely.

But Carol saw an odd glint appear in Jason's eyes for an instant. *He remembers something. Jason has a talent for becoming involved with weirdos. He isn't being honest . . .*

Eight

Ronnie slid down in her chair. When was that creep going to let them go? It seemed like ten hours since their meal break when she'd had a Western omelet and a chocolate shake at a greasy spoon down the street from the hotel, along with several other members of the training. They had insisted she couldn't go floating around the neighborhood by herself at this hour. Charlie – the guy who was head of the big talent agency – had even insisted on paying her check.

A woman had the mike now. She was a college professor, somewhere in her late forties, who had been married briefly during graduate school. She'd had a baby, a daughter she'd given up for adoption. She was agonizing over a recently ended ten-year lesbian relationship.

"You don't know how to love!" the trainer interrupted. "You're throwing out a lot of bullshit."

For ten minutes he chastised the college professor with a vulgarity that made the woman cringe, yet she clung to every word. Then suddenly he was dismissing the group. They were to return tomorrow morning at eight-thirty sharp.

"I don't want to hear any crap about your being too tired to come! Pull your asses together and get here."

Ronnie went to the line-up of phones and called Daddy to come and get her. It was two a.m. In six-and-a-half hours she had to be back here. But she wasn't coming back, no matter what Daddy said.

She waited in the vicinity of the check-in desk until her father walked into the lobby. She had been fighting to keep from falling asleep, but the minute she saw him she was wide awake again. Driving home she spilled forth her recriminations about AMO.

"Baby, I know." Jason refused to be angry. "I felt the same way the first day. But tomorrow you'll get into the real training. I won't tell you what's going to happen, but you'll feel great afterwards. Now you'll begin to live."

He kept talking all the way home. He was still spewing forth praise of AMO when they parked the car in the apartment garage and headed for the elevators.

"Honey, remember not to tell your mother one word about AMO," he reminded in the elevator. "She'd be negative about it just because *I* put you into it. Our secret." He swatted her on the rump with a conspiratorial smile.

"Yeah, Daddy." But she wasn't going back to that over-sized padded cell tomorrow morning. She was going to bed to sleep for twelve hours straight.

How could all those creeps get up and spill their guts that way? She hadn't opened her mouth. But it might be fun, she thought with unexpected amusement, to get up and pour out some way-out story about nobody loving her and how she was dying for affection. Nobody was ever supposed to repeat anything they heard in the training. She could have them all crying for her in three minutes, she gloated. A real show-stopper.

Ronnie thought they were alone in the apartment until

her father kissed her good-night at her bedroom door. But as his mouth brushed her cheek, she spied the den door open a fraction of an inch and close again. *Tiger was here.* Over Jason's shoulder she searched the living room, spied Tiger's five-inch-heeled Charles Jourdan shoes, which she invariably kicked off when she walked into the apartment.

"Good-night, Daddy." Ronnie was wistful, sweet. Inside she churned with rage.

She closed the bedroom door, stripped naked and, without bothering even to wash her face, slid between the sheets. In moments she was asleep.

"You goddamn bitch!" Daddy's voice roared into her head. "Don't tell me what to do!"

Instantly she was wide awake. She sat upright in bed – listening to the battle between Daddy and Tiger. Why didn't they fight in the studio? That was soundproofed.

"Don't you dare hit me!" Tiger shrieked.

Ronnie leapt from the bed. Trembling with a blend of exhaustion and excitement, she fumbled in the closet for the sheer black nightie and peignoir Daddy had bought for her in Paris. It had cost a fortune. She pulled the nightie over her creamy white nakedness, pulled on the peignoir while she hurried in bare feet to the door.

Tiger was screaming with the precision of a machine gun and Daddy was throwing furniture around the room. Ronnie hoped the people downstairs were away for the weekend.

"You bastard!" Tiger yelled in pain. "You'll kill me!"

"You don't deserve to live!" Daddy roared. "What do you mean, telling me you don't want to record Eddie's new song? I make the decisions around here!"

Why don't they go into the studio before somebody calls 911?

They were moving out of the den into the living room, Ronnie realized.

"Don't you dare throw that TV at me!" Tiger screeched.

Ronnie cracked the bedroom door. Tiger was at the sofa, trying to get into her clothes. Her face was streaked with mascara, her jaw swollen. Wearing only jockey shorts Daddy stood in the doorway to the den, his face flushed with rage. His arms showed rips from Tiger's fingernails. His thighs were scratched and bleeding.

"Jason," Tiger whimpered, struggling into her shoes. "We're going to record Monday night? The date's set?"

"Yeah. We'll record," he conceded. "Now get the hell out of here before I change my mind."

Tiger left the apartment. Jason moved over behind the bar, pulled out the ice cubes, and looked about with a scowl. "Where the hell is the Chivas Regal?"

Ronnie closed the door again but remained there, listening to the sounds in the living room. She was glad Daddy had beaten up Tiger. She deserved it. Nobody was better than Daddy when it came to the music business. If he said they ought to record a song, that meant it was sure to make the charts. Daddy's office wall was lined with golden CDs.

Daddy was drinking a lot. But she'd never seen him really zonked.

"Shit, no more ice cubes. To hell with it," he announced to the furniture. "Who needs it?"

Carefully Ronnie opened the door an inch. Daddy was heading for the studio. She watched him go inside. He left the door open and moments later punk rock – at an

70

open-air-concert volume – rent the air. They'd be able to hear it all the way out in California!

Ronnie darted out into the living room, running on cat-quiet feet to the studio. Daddy was in the control room.

"Daddy?" Her heart was pounding.

Jason swung about to face her. His eyes were glazed, his face still flushed. "Hey, baby, you ought to be asleep."

"Let me turn off the tape," she soothed. "Somebody'll call the cops if you keep that concert going," she jibed with her limpid, baby stare.

"Pretty baby," he crooned, then winced. "Christ, I feel lousy."

"Lie down on the chaise," she ordered, leaning forward to guide him to the black velvet-covered chaise in the studio, where he liked to sprawl and listen to tapes.

"God, I feel lousy," he groaned while she helped him stretch out.

"You'll feel better in a few minutes," she promised, massaging the back of his neck the way he'd taught her to.

"Pretty baby," he murmured. "Pretty baby."

She left him snoring on the chaise and went back to bed. Okay, she thought, she would go to the training session tomorrow. Daddy would be angry if she didn't.

She saw the first streaks of gray dawn filter through the drapes; she wouldn't sleep now. She'd got her second wind. In a little while she'd get up, dress, make coffee. Daddy wanted her to go through this shit-training. Okay, she'd do it. She'd do anything he wanted. *Didn't he know that?*

At seven-thirty she got out of bed and went to the closet. No jeans and t-shirt today. She picked out the Armani

71

dress that Daddy said made her look twenty. Wouldn't Charlie's eyes pop out when he saw her today!

At eight, dressed and with a coffee mug in hand, she went into the studio. Daddy lay face down on the chaise.

"Daddy . . ." Her eyes were bright with anticipation. *How much did he remember about last night?* "I've brought you coffee."

"It's chilly in here," he mumbled, unfamiliarly self-conscious. His eyes were wary. *He isn't sure what had happened last night.* "Bring me a robe, will you, baby?"

"Sure."

She put the mug on the floor beside the chaise and went into the bedroom to pull down one of the Gucci robes that hung at the left side of the closet wall. She returned to the den.

"God, I'm hung over," he groaned, sipping from the mug while still prone on his stomach.

"Put this on," she said with wide-eyed sweetness. "I'll hold your coffee.

He swung his legs to the floor, took the robe, pulled it on – tying the sash awkwardly about his waist.

"Daddy, are you going to take me to AMO or shall I just grab a cab?"

"I'll take you," he mumbled.

"No," she rejected with an air of triumph. "You go back to sleep. I'll grab a cab." Daddy always stuffed bills into her purse when she was with him.

He loves me more than Tiger.

Nine

Carol awoke to the sound of water pounding in the bathroom. Larry was showering. She put a hand out beside her – seeking comfort in the warm imprint of his body on the flowered sheet. Simultaneously she remembered she'd promised Max she would be back at the office today. Max had called to beg her to come back: "Carol, you know our crazy deadlines! We're way behind schedule. We need you to pull everything together."

She suspected that Larry had conspired with Donna to have Max call, but at the same time she realized that the office must be in chaos and the crew near panic as deadlines approached. In the course of time she'd become the linchpin that held Encore Magazines together – a fact which accounted for her decent raises these past three years.

But she wasn't ready to go back. She felt a tightening in the pit of her stomach at the prospect. *Why did I agree to come in today? It doesn't matter that I told Jason I'd be back at work today. So his fancy private investigator will call me there – the office could just say I was out at meetings. Donna could handle that. What can he do that Jenkins and Corelli can't do?*

"Carol?" A gentle protest in Larry's voice at the sight of her still in bed.

"I'll get up in a few minutes." She uttered a wistful sigh. "Larry, I don't want to go into the office just yet . . ." Her eyes pleaded with him to agree.

He ignored the plea. "I know, but it's important you do."

He crossed to sit at the edge of the bed, reached for her hand. "We'll cab uptown together. I'll meet you at six-thirty for dinner at Cosmos." The neighborhood restaurant at the corner of Second Avenue and Twenty-Third Street was somewhere they could relax.

Carol struggled for composure. God, she dreaded the outpouring of sympathy that would greet her at the office.

"All right." She managed a shaky smile. It would be no easier a week or a month from now. And she had bills to meet.

Larry pulled her close, rested his face against hers for a moment. "I know it'll be rough for you, but you have to get past this hurdle. Remember, I'm here for you. I'll always be here for you. Now go in and shower and dress. I'll make breakfast."

When Carol emerged from the shower, she sniffed the aroma of fresh coffee and was aware of hunger. For the first time since that awful day she was hungry. She recoiled from this realization. How could she feel hunger when her sweet, precious baby was gone?

She and Larry cabbed up Third Avenue together. He left the cab with her and walked her to the entrance of the building that housed Encore Magazines.

"You're going to handle this," he told her with conviction. "I'll be in the office all morning if you want to talk.

I have a long lunch with a client but then I'll return to the office." He kissed her tenderly, then headed north in the direction of his own workplace.

Trying to gear herself up for what lay ahead, Carol walked into the small, marble-floored lobby. In a corner of her mind she regarded returning to work as a desecration to Ronnie's memory. This was saying, "I had a rough time, but I'm putting the past behind me. I'm resuming my life as though nothing terrible happened."

She joined others waiting for the elevator. Did they know what had happened? The tabloids had splashed the story across the front pages once they realized Ronnie was Jason's daughter. She felt relief that no one seemed to recognize her. Every day, she thought bitterly, a new tragedy assaulted newspaper readers.

The elevator arrived at the lobby floor. The door opened. There was the usual rush inside. She was conscious of a tightness between her shoulder blades, at the nape of her neck. Her heart was pounding.

She waited for the elevator to arrive at her floor. The door opened; she walked into the lobby. Tina, the receptionist, rushed forward.

"Carol, we were all so shocked. Our hearts are with you . . ." Tina was an avid reader of their confession magazine. "But I know you're brave."

"Thank you, Tina."

She steeled herself not to break down as others rushed forward to offer condolences. Mercifully brief. She guessed that Donna had forewarned them. Donna knew how she dreaded this encounter.

Donna emerged from the Art Department, waved a greeting. Max flung open the door of his office, stood there – a squat, brawny character with a penchant for screaming at his employees.

"Thank God you're back." He greeted her with intentional brusqueness. At odd intervals he displayed an unexpected sensitivity. "I have to leave tonight for Texas – a meeting with our new printers." Max was forever in search of good deals. "You keep everybody on their toes – we're behind schedule. We've got deadlines to meet!"

"I'll be a tyrant," she promised. It was unreal, she thought, to come back and perform as though her life had not been destroyed.

At ten sharp, as Jason had said, Lou Henderson called. Donna summoned her from a conference with the Art Department. She was tempted to have Donna say she was out, but Jason would pester her until she saw this creep.

"I'll take it in my office, Donna."

She listened with strained politeness while Lou Henderson introduced himself.

"Mr Henderson, I don't know why Jason is going through this. There's nothing I can tell you that the police don't already know."

"I've just learned something the police don't know," Henderson said quietly. "Though I've convinced Mr Evans they must be informed immediately."

Her heart began to pound. "You know who killed Ronnie?"

"Not yet, but the suspect list has just broadened. I'd like to talk with you this evening."

She hesitated a moment. "I'll be home by eight," she said. What had Jason told this man that the police didn't know? That *she* didn't know? She'd been so sure she knew everything about Ronnie's activities. *As her mother I should have known!*

As soon as she was off the phone with Henderson, she called Larry. He was in conference with a client.

"Shall he call you back, Carol?" his secretary asked.

"No. Thank you, no. It isn't important." She would tell Larry at dinner. It was selfish to interrupt his business day with this.

She flung herself into the backlog of work that had pyramided in her absence. At regular intervals Lou Henderson's voice ricocheted through her mind. Had he learned something about the two hundred thousand dollars? How long had that money been hidden in Ronnie's closet? Why was it there?

She had lunch with Max in his office from paper bags brought up from the deli, while they discussed a possible one-shot on Monica Lewinsky. It was almost as though she had not been away. Except that she had to go home tonight knowing Ronnie was not there to greet her with her sweet, vivacious smile and a montage of the day's happenings.

She left the office promptly at six, walked east to Second Avenue for the southbound bus. What had Jason tried to keep from the police? *I know something the police don't know. Though I've convinced Mr. Evans that they must be informed.* At least Henderson was ethical.

Larry was waiting for her in their favorite booth at Cosmos. His eyes were guarded while he listened to her report about Henderson. He was weighing the possibility that this might be some devastating revelation, she told herself. How like Jason to try to hide something that might be important.

"Larry, what do you suppose this is?"

"We'll know soon." His smile was casual. "You told Henderson we'd be home by eight?"

"Right."

A few minutes before eight they were at the apartment door. Carol went into the tiny dressing room to change into slacks and shirt. As she emerged, she heard the intercom buzz. Henderson had arrived.

Larry opened the door for the investigator. He was a well-dressed, low-key man in his late forties, with the air of efficiency that Jason demanded of those – other than artists – who served him.

"You made a disconcerting statement on the phone," she said without preliminaries after she had introduced him to Larry.

"May I sit down?" he asked and Carol felt color tinge her cheekbones. Jason had probably told him about Larry's role in her life.

"Please do." Her eyes clung to him.

"I understand Mr Evans never revealed to you that your daughter took two weekends of AMO training recently," Henderson began.

"I don't know what you're talking about." Carol stared at him.

"You've heard about AMO," Larry reminded her. "It's getting a lot of promotion. A kind of group therapy on a massive scale."

Carol gaped in shock. "Ronnie never said a word . . ."

"Mr Evans took the training and was so impressed he wanted his daughter to take it, too." Henderson was speaking in a detached fashion that, illogically, infuriated her. "He said he had kept it a secret because he was afraid you'd disapprove."

"What has AMO training got to do with Ronnie's murder?" Her voice was harsh with the effort not to lash out at Henderson. She could hear Jason talking in the charismatic voice that mesmerized recording artists into signing with him: *'Our secret, baby. Be sure you don't tell your mother.'* That was Jason's style. "I don't understand, Mr. Henderson . . ."

"We're convinced Ronnie was murdered by someone who knew her. We have to run down every possible individual with whom she had contact," Henderson said with a new briskness. "Re-create her activities the week before her death."

"You're going to question all the other people in the AMO training group?" Larry lifted one eyebrow in doubt.

"I'll try to cut it down," Henderson conceded, "but we must follow every possible trail." At how much per day? Carol asked herself. "I was disappointed to discover that the young lady Mr Evans felt was his daughter's closest friend is no longer available for questioning."

"Cindy Weinberg?" Alarm brushed her. "She . . . she's all right?"

"Oh yes," Henderson reassured her. "But her mother took her out of school early and rushed her off to Europe. I wonder why she did that?" In contrast to the detachment in his voice his eyes were appraising.

"Cindy was distraught," Carol told him. He obviously suspected Cindy knew something. What could she have known? About the AMO training, her mind pinpointed. There was nothing Cindy and Ronnie had not told each other.

"There's a young man, too, who was a close friend. Paul Martin. He lives in this building, doesn't he?"

"On the floor above," Larry contributed.

"I'd like to talk to him."

"Why?" Carol recoiled from this. "He's told the police everything he can. Ask them. Don't bother Paul."

Carol saw the hesitancy in Lou Henderson's eyes and braced herself for an unexpected thrust.

"Mrs Evans, could Ronnie have had any drug connections?"

"Absolutely not!" Rage threatened her composure. What was this creep trying to do? "That's a dead end."

"I ask only because of the cache of money in the closet," Henderson pointed out.

"Ask your client about that." Carol's eyes blazed. "I can't believe Jason has nothing to do with that."

"I have no legal grounds for questioning the Martin boy," Henderson returned to his earlier quarry, "but it might prove immensely helpful. It would be easier if you asked him to come down here."

"You mean he might talk more freely away from his mother," Larry pinpointed.

"Exactly. He might be reluctant to discuss information that might involve himself with her present."

"Paul Martin is one of the finest kids I've ever known," Carol shot back. "I was delighted Ronnie had him for a friend."

"He'll know about Ronnie's activities these last weeks," Henderson pursued. "He might give us a lead."

"Carol, call him," Larry encouraged. "This isn't a police matter."

Reluctantly she went to the phone and called Paul. He

was in the midst of homework, he said, but he agreed to come downstairs to talk to Henderson. He sounded uneasy.

"He'll be right down," Carol reported. *Why did I call him? Hasn't he been through enough?*

She was so sure she had known where Ronnie was every minute. But Ronnie had kept the two weekends of AMO training from her. What else? *No, I won't think this way. It's Jason's fault, damn him! Jason forced Ronnie to be deceptive.*

Ten

Lou Henderson asked a flood of questions about Ronnie's school. Carol answered with a succinctness that she knew exasperated him, but she was caught up in the revelation of the AMO weekends. Ronnie hated all therapy. Why had she gone along with this?

Carol shivered, suddenly thrust back into those nightmare years of psychologists and psychiatrists, before she had conceded that therapy was useless because Ronnie invariably lied. But in the last two years Ronnie had seemed to improve immeasurably. No more screaming tantrums, no more physical encounters where she scratched and pummeled her mother.

God, the times Ronnie had refused to go to an appointment and Carol had had to pay for nothing! She flinched, reliving with devastating clarity the six weeks of behavior modification which had been so humiliating for both Ronnie and her. She remembered the last psychiatrist who, when Ronnie balked against any more therapy and had refused to go to his office, had offered to make house calls at two hundred and fifty dollars an hour. *How could Jason have persuaded Ronnie to buy the AMO bit?*

Two weekends. Carol knew exactly which they were – the two weekends when she'd been a nervous wreck because Ronnie hadn't come home until three a.m. Jason had called from up in Connecticut the first weekend – so he'd claimed – to say they were in some village without a service station, the car had broken down, and she wasn't to worry but they'd probably be terribly late. She had hung at the window, watching for Jason's car until it finally pulled up at the curb and Ronnie jumped out.

The second weekend Jason had called – supposedly from a phone booth on the Merritt Parkway – to say he was taking Ronnie for dinner up in Connecticut and she was not to worry if they were late. Again, it had been past three a.m. when he brought Ronnie home. She had been livid; Ronnie had to be at school at nine. Ronnie had explained that they had gone back to the house to pick up her gear and were stuck in the elevator for hours.

"Oh, Mom, it was awful," she'd said dramatically. "Daddy and I were sitting on the floor waiting for the repair men to come and get us out. We couldn't even pee!"

What had really happened on those weekends? Did they have anything to do with Ronnie's murder? She searched her mind for answers . . .

Ronnie went to the second day of training with the knowledge that Daddy would not be seeing Tiger until the following night, when Tiger would be recording with the new group Daddy had put together. Ronnie was almost happy to be here with the now-familiar faces which yesterday had seemed so boring.

Everybody signed a statement again, promising not to tell anybody how the training was conducted and to repeat nothing that was said by the trainees. They

83

wouldn't, she guessed with fresh awareness. They were all mesmerized. Wow, she'd love to get this on tape, but the first day they got the word – no tape recorders. Now she understood why.

Most of the real training came through next weekend. Today was so dull. But it was wild the way some of these characters spilled out their guts. She listened to the fifty-year-old investment counselor in front of her – Doug, his name tag read – whose strong, forceful wife had died eight months ago and who was now at a loss to manage his own life.

"I told myself I loved my wife," he said, "but I hated her for managing everything. She decided where we went on vacations, who our friends would be. She even decided what nights we could have sex. She emasculated me!"

Somebody to the left waved a hand, signaling he wanted a vomit bag. A moment later two other hands shot up. To the background of retching the investment counselor listened to the trainer blast him for his inadequacies. This crap was enough to make anybody throw up, Ronnie thought with distaste.

With an eerie sense of exhilaration she indicated she wanted the microphone. This was like a drug high, she thought, rising to her feet. She was glad she'd worn the Armani dress. It made her look older.

"Nobody has ever truly loved me," Ronnie began, her voice poignant, her face heartbreakingly wistful. "They didn't want me. My parents married in high school because they had to. Sometimes I wish my mother had gone for an abortion. My mother was too lazy even to change my diapers. When I was six years old and going to school, I had to wash my clothes if I wanted something clean to wear the next day. Mom was conked out all day in front of the TV, and Daddy was screwing anybody who'd give him a chance. Even when Daddy started making lots of money, they didn't have time for me. Mom was forever at Bergdorf's or Bloomie's and Daddy was always running out of town on business trips."

She stood there with a beautiful sense of importance as she continued to weave her fantasy. They were all listening to her. Charlie had tears in his eyes. A woman up front sobbed aloud. She didn't hear the trainer ripping her to shreds. She was feeling all this love welling up for her. *Amo, amas, amat. But I love only Daddy.*

At last they were given their pee break and meal break. When she came out of the restroom, Ronnie was surprised to find Charlie waiting to take her to dinner. He really believed all that garbage she'd thrown at them. All at once she was determined to see Charlie outside of AMO.

While they ate, she wistfully apologized for having been so frank about her parents.

"But that's why you're in the training," Charlie soothed.

"I get so sore at Daddy, but I still love him. Here I am, eighteen years old," she lied, "and I still feel so tied to my folks. Daddy's birthday is next week. Charlie, can I ask you a big favor? I want to buy Daddy a special present – I mean, I feel so bad about sharing the way I did." She took a deep breath. "Would you meet me at Saks tomorrow and help me pick out a wallet for him?"

"I can't do it tomorrow." Charlie frowned in thought. "What about Tuesday?"

"Tuesday would be super, Charlie." She glowed with gratitude, masking her disappointment. She wanted to be with Charlie tomorrow evening when Daddy was with Tiger.

Ronnie and Charlie ate hastily and returned to the hotel. She hoped they wouldn't be stuck here forever. Mom expected her home by six. Daddy was going to call up and alibi her. She hoped he wouldn't forget.

Mom was waiting up when she let herself into the apartment. She looked dragged out, grim.

"It's past three, Ronnie. I don't know how you're going to school tomorrow."

"I'll cut my first two classes," Ronnie said calmly. "I won't miss anything."

She slept till noon, got up and made herself breakfast and went back to sleep. Cindy called her at a little past three to ask about the weekend. All the while they talked Ronnie was remembering that Daddy would be seeing Tiger tonight. After a session the whole mob always went out somewhere together. Would he bring Tiger back home with him? Sure he would.

"Cindy, it was wild. We're going through this eyeball-to-eyeball routine, and this closet lesbian next to me falls dead in a faint and people all around me are bawling. You wouldn't believe it."

Cindy and she talked for almost two hours, then she went in to shower. She was drying her hair with the super-max when the phone rang. It was Mom.

"Ronnie, I'm going to be stuck at the office until at least ten," Carol apologized. She always felt guilty when she had to work late. "Take some money from the cookie jar and buy yourself a barbecued chicken and salad. All right?"

"Sure, no sweat."

She wouldn't bother going down for the chicken. There was always something in the fridge to defrost. Anyhow, she wasn't hungry now. Just restless. She glanced at the clock. The recording session was called for eight. Almost three hours yet.

She'd listen to CDs for a while, then she'd eat. She lay across the bed with music filling the bedroom, but her mind roved to Tiger. Tiger wasn't like Daddy's other women. She was older, smarter. Tiger knew what Daddy could do for her. Even when he beat her up, Tiger wanted to be sure he was still going to record her. Daddy could make her a superstar. But maybe he wouldn't.

She wandered between bedroom and kitchen – snacking, not bothering with a solid meal, listening to music. At ten minutes to eight she called her father. She felt a compulsion to hear his voice, to remind him of her presence.

"Hello." Jason sounded irritated at the intrusion.

"Daddy . . ." It was her nymphette-in-heat voice.

"Baby, we're getting ready for a session," he told her brusquely. "You know that."

"I thought you were recording at eight." She was apologetic. "I just wanted to know if you thought I ought to go to the mid-week training on Wednesday night. Cindy'll cover for me." Mid-week they'd cut early.

"Jason, honey . . ." Tiger's powerful voice, lowered to a sultry undertone, filtered down the telephone line. It brought Ronnie's back up like a cornered Siamese. "You've got to do something about the room-tone here. It stinks!"

"Tiger, you're nuts," Jason rejected. "This is one of the hottest studios in town!"

They were in the control room, Ronnie noted. Daddy had picked up the extension in there. The engineer was checking the input.

"Look, baby, we're ready to go ahead," Jason told her. "I'll talk to you later in the week."

"Sure, Daddy." Ronnie slammed down the receiver. On impulse she dialed the Martins' apartment.

"Hello," Paul answered.

"What are you doing?" Her tone was wistful.

"I'm cramming for an algebra quiz," he reported. "If I don't come home with an A, my mother's going to have a fit. She's already worrying about my SATs."

"Maybe you need a break." That was what Mom told her whenever she got uptight about cramming for a test. "Come down and help me with my French."

"I don't think I'd better, Ronnie." But he sounded ambivalent.

"Is your mother home?"

"She took a cousin from out of town to dinner." But he was worried his mother might phone, Ronnie guessed.

"Leave the phone off the hook and come down here," Ronnie ordered. "You can tell them you were talking to somebody about a problem you couldn't solve and the 'call-waiting' wasn't working."

"Gee, I don't know." Still he hesitated.

"Look, we'll both take a twenty-minute break," she soothed. "I've got a new CD you haven't heard. A single that Daddy says will really break out."

"Okay," Paul capitulated. "I'll be right down. But just for twenty minutes."

Ronnie trailed out of the bedroom to the foyer. Tiger wasn't really crazy about Daddy. She just wanted to make

88

him think she was. Girl vocalists were forever throwing themselves at him.

The doorbell buzzed. Ronnie pulled it wide. Right away she sensed that Paul was depressed.

"Why didn't you bring Machiavelli with you?" she reproached. She adored that crazy dog.

"He was sleeping." Paul sighed, "I ought to be upstairs cramming for the quiz. Maybe if I flunk algebra Mom will switch me to another school." His eyes brightened.

"You still hate it that much?" She walked towards the bedroom. She never used Mom's stereo. It was cruddy compared to her own.

"I wish the school would burn down!" he said with sudden violence. "The guys are such a bunch of jocks."

"So you don't dig sports, so what?" Ronnie shrugged, pulling the new CD from the rack.

Paul was silent for a moment.

"So in their eyes that makes me gay," he blurted out. "They keep making cracks."

Ronnie stood still, CD in hand. "Are you?"

Paul blushed. Shit, by now he ought to be used to her saying whatever came into her mind. That showed him she thought he was a special friend. Like Cindy. She was always so sweet and polite to everybody else.

"No," he managed to deny.

"How do you know you're not?" she pushed. *Was Tiger screwing up the session? She hoped so.* "Did you ever try it?"

"Ronnie, you're weird!" He was disconcerted. She had never talked about sex with Paul. She had never talked about it with anybody at school, except Cindy.

Of course, they'd had sex education classes in school,

back in the sixth grade. But that wasn't where she'd got her real education. Last year, when Daddy was in London, she'd taken Cindy up to his apartment and they'd read all the sex manuals he kept hidden in the liquor cabinet. They looked at all the photographs but they hadn't run the videos because she was afraid of not getting them put away right.

Paul lowered himself onto one of the pair of huge pillows positioned against the radiator to listen to the CD. Ronnie draped herself across the foot of the bed.

"Paul, did you ever worry that maybe those creeps at school were right?" she asked with an air of tender solicitude. "Wouldn't you like to know for sure that you're not gay?"

"What do you mean?" Again color crept into his face. "I'm sure."

"In your head you wonder sometimes," she insisted, her eyes holding his.

"I won't go back to that school next year." His mouth was set. "I'll tell Mom."

"Your mother will get hysterical. She'll think something happened," Ronnie warned. "Don't change schools." Mrs Martin had moved him to the boys school because she heard about all the girls that got pregnant at Fairbanks last year.

"You don't know how awful it is." His face contorted in anguish.

"I'll prove you're not gay," Ronnie promised. She rose to her feet and pulled her t-shirt over her head, dropped it to the floor. She never wore a bra. "Paul . . ."

"Ronnie, your mother," he faltered.

"She won't be home for hours. Don't you like me?" She pretended to be hurt.

"Yes," he whispered. "You're beautiful."

"Then relax, silly," she whispered. In a few minutes Paul would know for sure he wasn't gay.

"Ronnie, put your t-shirt back on," he ordered with sudden strength. "Stop this weird game."

Eleven

The doorbell rang. "I'll get it," Larry said.

Carol sat at the edge of her chair. Why had she phoned Paul and asked him to come down here? Henderson would upset him with more questions. She should have refused.

"Thank you for coming, Paul," Larry said gently and prodded him into the living room. "This is Mr Henderson, a private investigator hired by Ronnie's father. He's trying to find Ronnie's killer. He'd like you to answer a few questions."

"Please sit down, Paul," Henderson told him.

"I can't stay long." Paul was scared. "I have homework to do. And I don't know if my mother would want me to talk to you," he added with shaky defiance.

"I'm sure your mother and you want Ronnie's killer captured," Larry said appeasingly.

"Yes, sir."

Paul was so pale, Carol thought. He shouldn't be questioned again.

"We'd like to know how much Ronnie told you about her AMO training," Henderson began.

Paul frowned. "I . . . I don't know what you're talking about."

"You were her close friend," Henderson chided. "Surely she talked a lot about it to you."

"She didn't say anything." Paul's eyes settled on the floor. "We talked about school . . . and things like that . . ."

"She never mentioned any of the people she met through the AMO training?" Henderson went on with an air of disbelief.

"I don't know anything about it. I never heard of AMO training." He rose to his feet. "If that's all you want to ask me, I have to go back to my homework."

"Thank you, Paul," Henderson said. "That's all I wanted to know."

Larry went to the door with Paul, locked it behind him.

"The kid's lying." Henderson squinted in thought.

"He's lying," Larry confirmed.

"Why?" Carol was bewildered. "Did he think he was protecting Ronnie? He must have known Ronnie was keeping it from me, but why lie about it now?"

"Did Jason notify the police about the AMO business?" Larry asked.

Henderson nodded. "I convinced him he had no alternative. But why was Paul Martin lying?"

"A quixotic loyalty towards Ronnie perhaps," Larry decided. "You know how kids are about their friends."

"I'll talk with the AMO people tomorrow," Henderson said. "That's a highly emotional situation. I want to track down any personal contacts Ronnie might have formed there."

"Do you expect them to talk to you?" Carol was skeptical. Why had *she* agreed to talk to Lou Henderson?

The police were not going to be happy that Jason had brought a private investigator into the case. But he had thrown her off balance with the AMO training.

"The AMO people will be cooperative," Henderson brought her back into the conversation. "It would be bad public relations for them to be connected with a murder. You figure how much money they take in each weekend?"

"You believe someone from the training may have killed Ronnie?" Carol was suddenly cold. How could Jason have thrown her into a situation like that?

"We have to consider every possibility," Henderson said. "Then there's the two hundred thousand dollars the police found in Ronnie's room . . ."

"Don't expect me to know anything about that," Carol bristled. "Talk to your client."

What were Jenkins and Corelli doing about that? Did they believe she'd hidden the money in Ronnie's closet?

Henderson cleared his throat, rose to his feet. "Thank you for seeing me, Mrs Evans."

Larry went to the door with Henderson, came back into the living room.

"Would you like more coffee?"

"Okay." Carol was churning with reproaches. Why had Jason involved Ronnie in that AMO mess? What had Ronnie said that might have driven someone to kill her? She started at the jangle of the telephone, went over to respond.

"Is Lou there?" Jason asked.

"He just left. That was a rotten thing to do!" Her temper flared. "Putting Ronnie into that crazy therapy behind my back! God knows what she ran into there!"

"Did you cooperate with Lou?" He ignored her recriminations. Carol heard a woman's voice in the background and Jason's abrupt reponse: "Tiger, will you hold it till I'm off the phone?"

"I spoke with Henderson." Carol struggled to regain her composure. She wouldn't give Jason the satisfaction of knowing how much he had upset her. It gave him a sense of power. "Don't send him here again. And don't call me, Jason. I want to forget I ever knew you." She hung up, shaking. The only thing Jason had ever given her was Ronnie – and Ronnie was dead.

Larry came to her, held out a mug of coffee. His eyes were tender.

"Sit down and relax," he told her.

"That's a large order." She managed a wry smile. "Talking to Jason always upsets me. He stirs up ugly memories."

"He's out of your life, Carol. Forget him." He sighed. "I know – that's hard right now."

"Larry, thank God for you." Her eyes told him she loved him, yet this wasn't their time. *Did he understand that?*

"You're a survivor," he reminded her. "You had the guts to get away from Jason." But his eyes were full of questions she couldn't answer.

"After Jason overdosed with his vocalist of the moment, I had no other recourse." She paused to sip the strong black coffee that was Larry's specialty. Her mind recreated that awful weekend with a clarity that turned her sick even now. "I walked into the studio. They were both out cold. Both stark naked. The damn syringes were lying beside them." She shivered in recall. "I ran to the phone, called for an ambulance – not realizing I left the door open behind me. Ronnie walked in on them. She was only five but she knew something awful had happened. She stood there screaming till I ran back and pulled her out of there. She wanted to ride in the ambulance with Jason. When he came home, she hung around his bed every moment – terrified he'd die. Then he flew off to Europe for six weeks with a new slut. I rented a fleabag apartment in Manhattan, furnished it through my charge plates. Jason was furious when he came home and discovered I'd left him. He didn't think I'd dare."

"You had to do it for Ronnie as well as yourself," Larry reminded her.

"But Ronnie never forgave me." Carol shook her head in frustration. "She hated every girl that Jason took up with but she never forgave me for divorcing him. She kept a scrapbook filled with every word she found published about Jason. The last item was about Jason and Tiger Rhodes." Carol shivered. "She hated that woman. But Larry, how did all that money get into Ronnie's closet?"

Ronnie had hidden the money for Jason. That had to be the answer . . .

Twelve

Ronnie struggled with the door keys. Damn these locks. The phone was ringing. With the locks opened, she flung the door wide and darted into her room. The phone was still ringing – probably Cindy, who must have just got home from school, too. She threw herself across the bed and picked up the receiver.

"Hi."

"Did you read this week's *Enquirer*?" Cindy demanded avidly.

"You know Mom won't let that in the house. Why?"

"There's a story about some girl singer – Tiger Rhodes – and a picture of her hanging on to your old man. She says they're having a fantastic relationship."

"Screw her," Ronnie said.

"Your old man's doing that," Cindy giggled.

"Shut up!" Ronnie ordered. "Just shut up." This relationship was different from the others. Tiger was sharp. She was using Daddy. Couldn't he see that? "Look, I've got to dress and go meet Charlie. I'll call you back later."

Ronnie deliberated a moment, then phoned Jason. He wasn't at the apartment. She tracked him to his office but had to hang on a few minutes before the receptionist put her through.

97

Julie Ellis

"Yeah, Ronnie." Jason sounded terse.

"Daddy, Cindy says there's a terrific photo of you in this week's *Enquirer*. Will you save me a copy? You know how Mom is about me reading the *Enquirer*." She was appealingly wistful.

"Sure, baby. We've got a dozen in the office." She'd known he would have.

"You didn't tell me there was going to be a story about you in the *Enquirer*," she pouted.

"It wasn't my story," he reminded. "Publicity for Tiger. We set this up to tie in with her CD. You know how important timing is. Look, baby, I have to get off . . ."

"I'm sorry I bothered you, Daddy." Her hurt was orchestrated to reach him.

"Ronnie, you didn't bother me," he objected. "You know I love to talk to you. But right now I'm up to my ass in trouble. I have to come up with two hundred thousand to get the IRS off my back."

"I'm sorry you're having trouble. I wish I could help. Can I see you tonight?" She used her wistful voice. "Could we have dinner up at the apartment? I can call Mom and say I'm having dinner at Cindy's. I'll be at the training all weekend. I won't see you hardly at all."

"I wish I had the time, but no way. I have to talk to some people about raising that bread."

"I've decided to go to the mid-week training tomorrow night. Are you pleased?" The mid-week training was optional.

"That's great, honey. Look, we'll talk Friday night," he cajoled, clearly anxious to be off the phone. *Was Tiger there hanging over his shoulder?* "Okay?"

"Sure, Daddy."

98

Ronnie changed into a skirt and blouse that, combined with artful make-up, made her look at least eighteen. She put her hair up in a French twist, the way Donna had taught her but which Mom disliked and borrowed a pair of her mother's highest-heeled sandals that brought her up to model height. She checked her watch. She had a whole hour before she was to meet Charlie at Saks. She'd go up to look at the Calvin Kleins. If she liked something, they'd hold it till Daddy came over to buy it for her.

Was Daddy really in bad money trouble? Maybe she'd better not ask them to hold anything for her at Saks. He said the IRS wanted him to pay up two hundred thousand dollars. Daddy made a lot of money, but he blew it like it was confetti. Sometimes people went to jail for trying to screw the IRS. Was that why Daddy was so worried?

He was running around trying to raise the money, she convinced herself. That was why he couldn't see her. If he had the money, everything would be cool again.

Ronnie left the apartment, took the Third Avenue bus up to Forty-Ninth Street. At Forty-Ninth Street she left the bus and headed west, walking with small, slow steps because the heels of the sandals were unfamiliarly high. But high heels were sexy. She was aware of covert – and overt – glances of masculine admiration as she moved along the crowded street. Nobody here would ever guess she was only fourteen.

She went into Saks via the Forty-Ninth Street entrance, took the elevator upstairs to look at the new Calvin Kleins. She was flattered that the saleswoman recognized her but she refused to try anything on.

"I have to meet a friend downstairs." She gave the saleswoman a conspiratorial smile.

She spied Charlie waiting for her. He was inspecting the wallets. Charlie was a VIP, just as important as Daddy. But Daddy was too busy to let her come up to his apartment for dinner. His housekeeper left at six — he didn't like people around in the evenings. If he was having dinner at home, he called out. *Was he really in trouble with the IRS?*

"Hi." She greeted Charlie with a breathy eagerness.

"Hi, Ronnie. I've been looking at the wallets." He was self-conscious because the salesman was politely standing by. Adding up Charlie and her, Ronnie guessed, though he was too bright to let on what he was thinking.

"Which one should I take?"

For a few moments they concentrated on the wallets. Charlie respected the fact that she was buying from limited resources. Daddy always slipped her a fifty dollar bill when he took her home. "Don't tell your Mom," was his usual admonition. She'd give the wallet to Paul for his birthday next week. Wouldn't he be surprised?

"This one, please," she decided when Charlie had narrowed the choice down to two. While the salesman left them to process the transaction, Ronnie turned to Charlie. "You're so sweet," she murmured, but her mind was on a see-saw. *Was Daddy in trouble with the IRS? Was he scared they were going to arrest him for income tax evasion?* "I mean, to go to all this bother for me."

Charlie glowed, gratified by this reaction. Yet she sensed his inner conflict, his insecurity. She remembered him standing up in the training and saying to them all: 'Look at me. I'm fifty years old. I head a talent agency that controls half the personalities on TV. I can make or break the careers of some of the biggest names on the networks. I'm a VIP and I feel like shit.'

"It's too late to go back to the office," he said with an effort at casualness. "Would you like to drop in somewhere for a drink?"

"I'd love it." Nobody would ask her age, would they? For a moment she was intimidated. No. With Charlie she wouldn't have to worry about anything so silly. They'd just take it for granted that he wouldn't be out with a fourteen-year-old. They'd figure she was legal drinking age. "I was hoping you'd ask me."

"Then let's go." His face brightened. "As soon as you have your wallet wrapped."

Ronnie welcomed the muted lighting of the bar. Gradually she relaxed. Nobody was asking questions. She sipped at her white wine while Charlie told her about his ugly third divorce. She could play this game with no sweat.

"Christ, that woman was a bitch! She was the one who sent me to AMO. Cold as a dead fish."

In a minute Charlie was going to ask her up to his apartment. Her mind was racing. She knew how to help Daddy. *It's wild – but it'll work.*

"Do you like pop art?" Charlie asked.

"Some of it." Art wasn't her *schtick*, but she could go along with this.

"My last wife spent a fortune in the Fifty-Seventh Street galleries. I fought to hold on to every piece she bought," he said with satisfaction. "Why the hell should I let her walk out with what cost me nearly ninety thousand dollars? Would you like to see it?" He made it sound an impulsive invitation.

"Sure," she accepted. "I'd like to see what cost ninety thousand dollars."

They left the bar and cabbed to Charlie's plush Sutton Place apartment. In the cab he was already touching her. He was sure he'd have her flat on her back five minutes after they were in his apartment.

"Charlie, I'm glad you came to AMO," she whispered while they waited for the elevator. She leaned towards him, knowing the movement gave him a choice view of her cleavage. With the top three buttons open this blouse was almost as sexy as her Calvin Klein. "I like important men. They make me feel sexy."

"Do you feel sexy now?" His face was flushed with anticipation.

The elevator door opened. He jumped away from her. Two sternly girdled women with poodles emerged. Charlie prodded her into the elevator. Before the door was fully closed, he slid a hand inside her blouse.

"Charlie, that feels so good." Her eyes told him she couldn't wait to fall into bed with him. But he was still insecure. "And I'm not a cold fish."

The elevator slid to a stop. He propelled her out onto the lush carpeting of the corridor. His arm crept about her waist while they walked to the door of his apartment. She read the name-plate: Charles R. Reid. At AMO he was simply Charlie.

"Hey, I like this," she approved when he ushered her into the marble-floored foyer that was almost as large as their living room. She was sure the antiques in the foyer and the sweeping living room beyond were authentic. Where did he hang the pop art his third wife bought? Ronnie suppressed a giggle. Probably in the john.

"Nobody's here," he reassured her. "The couple who come in leave at three. Let me show you the master bedroom." His gaze was stripping her to skin.

"Yes, master," she flipped.

The master bedroom was impressive. Charlie made a lot of money. He'd been making it for a long time. Her eyes skimmed the ornate, carved wood ceiling, the elegant antique chests, the dramatic Sjorz bed covered with a Spanish rug. The windows were masked by a wall of Irish linen drapes, striped in royal blue, turquoise, and heliotrope. The same material covered the chaise in front of them.

"This wasn't decorated by your third wife," Ronnie joshed.

"An over-priced decorator," Charlie conceded, pulling off his jacket and loosening his tie.

Ronnie dropped to the chaise and settled herself along its length.

"Don't you want to get into something more comfort-able?" she challenged. He was nervous again.

"What about you?" he countered. He was staring hard at her.

"You come back out," she promised. "And I'll be very comfortable."

Charlie went into the master bathroom. Ronnie pulled off her sandals, stripped to bikini panties, and crossed to lie on the Spanish rug that covered the bed. She looked like one of those girls in *Playboy*, she told herself.

Charlie walked out of the bathroom, a silk robe tied loosely about his large frame. She watched while Charlie dropped the robe on the floor beside the bed.

"You're gorgeous." He climbed awkwardly beside her.

"I like broad-shouldered men. They're so macho." Her eyes settled on his chest. She made a mental note of the two-inch scar above one nipple and the mole on his left hip. "I like men with hair on their chest."

"What else do you like?" he drawled.

"Charlie, I think I owe it to you to tell the truth," she said, sweetly apologetic. "I lied when I said I was eighteen. I'm fourteen."

Charlie blanched. His face sagged. She was under the age of consent. He could be hauled in on a rape charge.

"Oh my God!" He stared at her in horror.

"Oh, don't worry, Charlie," she hastened to reassure him – dizzy with triumph. "It's going to be all right. I won't tell anybody. Not as long as you do exactly what I tell you."

Thirteen

S tifling a yawn Larry strode from the elevator, across the reception area and down the hall towards the corner office. He was barely making it through each day and had realized he was suffering from sleep deprivation. He hadn't had a decent night's rest in the three weeks he'd been sleeping on that lumpy sofa bed. How much longer before this affected his performance on the job? he asked himself uneasily. He prided himself on being a conscientious – sometimes over-zealous – architect.

Carol, too, had slept little these past two weeks since she'd rejected sleeping pills. She was fearful of becoming addicted. She tried so hard not to disturb him, prowling about the living room in bare feet, but they'd become so close that he knew the moment she left the bed.

He'd hoped that returning to the office would help her through these agonizing days and nights. Without his work he would have been a basket case in those early days after Betsy and David died. And he worried, too, that she would withdraw from the rest of the world – as he had done for years – once the working hours were past.

"Good morning." His administrative assistant greeted him with a blend of cheerfulness and an awareness that these were not good mornings for him.

"Hi, Deirdre." He forced a smile. "Any calls yet?"

"Just two." She handed him some notes. "Shall I call and reserve a table for dinner at—"

"Dinner?" Larry stared blankly for a moment. "Oh Lord, this is the day I'm having dinner with those two guys from Boston!" He'd forgotten about them. He had all the statistics ready to show, he'd just forgotten about the dinner appointment. "Give them a buzz to check on what time they'd like to meet. Then the usual – reserve a table at Michael's, call them back and confirm."

He sat at his desk, focused on the two calls he had to make. But first he needed to phone Carol. He'd be late again getting to the apartment. He punched in the number of her private line at her office.

"Carol Evans." Her voice so bright when he knew how she was hurting.

"Hi, honey. I totally forgot, I have a dinner meeting with two prospective clients in town from Boston," he apologized.

"Okay . . ." An uncertainty in her voice now. He knew she dreaded being alone in the apartment.

"Why don't you buzz Iris, see if she's clear tonight? The two of you go out to dinner somewhere special. My treat." He was trying to be casual.

"I'll call her," Carol promised. "How late do you think you'll be?"

"I imagine we'll break up by ten," he surmised.

"If Iris and I do go out for dinner, I'll be home by then."

Off the phone Larry sat motionless, staring into space, his mind in turmoil. Why couldn't he convince Carol to move in with him? They would be so much more

106

comfortable in his place, but more importantly she needed to get away from the apartment. At every turn she was confronted by memories. *I've been through that scene. I know her pain.*

I know it can't happen right away, but I can but see a good life ahead of us. Maybe even a family. We're both young enough for that. But I must be careful – Carol, so fragile. I must be patient. I mustn't jump the gun.

Carol remained at the office until a few minutes past seven – not a rare deal for her, though this evening the extra hour was unnecessary. She hadn't called Iris; she recoiled from the prospect of going out to dinner. That felt like a betrayal of Ronnie.

The only person still at the office was a member of the art department. She went in to tell him good-night, and headed for the elevator. Ronnie always liked to go out somewhere for dinner – though her taste reached beyond what their budget allowed. She'd come home from weekends with Jason and brag about going to expensive restaurants; the Union Square Cafe, the Four Seasons, Lespinasse. Should she have insisted that Ronnie stay in the parochial school – where there'd been after-school activities – instead of transferring to that expensive private school Jason chose? He paid the bills – how could she have objected?

But in the school she'd attended these past three years Ronnie had run with kids whose parents were wealthy. Cindy lived in a million dollar co-op. Even in their own building Paul and his mother lived in a two-bedroom apartment plus formal dining room. That more than doubled their rent. Ronnie was always unhappy about not having a charge account at Bloomie's or her own credit card. But on her salary – plus three hundred a month in child support – Carol couldn't afford that lifestyle.

This was the time of day she dreaded most, she thought, when she left the Second Avenue bus and headed for the apartment. Each time she unlocked the apartment door she was faced with the unassailable fact that never again would Ronnie be there, waiting for her to prepare dinner, hoping this would be an evening when she'd say, 'Okay, let's live dangerously and eat out tonight.'

Ronnie had been so bubbly, so avid for new adventures, and yet so vulnerable. *How had all that money come to be in her bedroom? She had to be covering in some insane way for Jason.*

Carol arrived at the house just as Iris emerged from a taxi.

"Hi." Iris hurried to join her. "You're working late again."

"A bit late," Carol conceded. Iris knew how often she worked late. Max had a habit of calling her in for a long conference just as she was leaving for the day, no matter that she had a young daughter waiting at home. She could hear him now: *'Carol, come in and let's toss around an idea I've got for a one-shot.'* "Larry has a dinner meeting with some prospective clients – I was in no rush to get home."

"Come up and have dinner with me," Iris coaxed. "I've got some chicken cutlets that I should use up. I'll toss on some herbs and they'll grill in three minutes in the new electric grill I picked up. Throw a couple of Idahoes in the microwave, steam some vegetables and voila – dinner in a few minutes."

"I have something I can pull out of the freezer," Carol hedged.

"Pull it out another night," Iris ordered. "Come up and keep me company."

"Thanks," Carol capitulated. For a little while she'd escape the intolerable act of walking into her own apartment alone. She managed a wisp of a smile. "It sounds great."

Iris had a two-bedroom, two-bathroom apartment. "For the rare occasions when Tim and Bob are home," she'd told Carol, but with both of them attending Californian universities that wasn't often. "I think they wanted to get as far away from their father as they could," she'd added.

When the two women were seated at the dining area table the conversation inevitably turned to the discovery of the duffel bag stuffed with money, and the lack of progress in tracking down Ronnie's killer.

"Jason keeps insisting he knows nothing about the money," Carol seethed. "He's trying to dump that on Ronnie's head. I didn't expect him to be that rotten."

"Honey, you know he's a bastard," Iris reminded. "Like my ex." She shook her head in frustration. "After four years I still can't believe Hank could have been such a heel. We'd been married twenty-three years. We had two sons, and he stared me straight in the eye and said, 'I never should have married you. You were just a convenience'."

"You're well rid of him." Carol was somber. She was so wrapped up in her own problems she'd forgotten how rough these years had been for Iris.

"I tell myself that." Iris managed a defiant smile. "And each year is a little better than the one before. But I've never been able to totally erase him from my consciousness. I hear a piece of music we both loved, see an old movie on TV that we saw together years ago, and I forget for a moment that he's out of my life."

"You've built a whole new life for yourself." *Will I ever be able to do that?* "You had the courage to walk out on a job you hated and move into a new career. Iris, you deserve enormous respect for what you've accomplished since your divorce."

Iris shrugged. "You mean my erotic hystericals? What's so great about that?"

"You support yourself in a comfortable lifestyle, without alimony."

"The days of decent alimony went out with women's lib. But I made sure Hank was committed to seeing Tim and Bob through school."

"Along with hefty loans," Carol reminded. Jason would have seen Ronnie through college – but that would never be now. "Tim will be out of law school in another year, won't he? And Bob still has a year to go on his MBA?"

Iris nodded. "It's a miracle Hank came through with the college money. The kids are still furious with him – they barely speak. Of course Hank blames that on me, says I turned them against him." She paused, her face tightening. "I didn't tell you his big news yet. It's tough for me to deal with . . ."

"What news?" Carol was startled.

"He called me three days ago. His new wife is pregnant. He thought Bob and Tim should know they'd have a

110

half-brother in six months. Isn't that cool?" Iris drawled. "That makes him feel like a prize stud."

"When Bob was here for part of his spring break, he said 'You know, my Mom is the very best'."

Iris grimaced. "I was a working mother. Guilt-ridden as hell. I tried to tell myself that bringing in money was important. That's how we kept that fancy house up in Westchester, a great place to raise kids. We took the kids to Europe twice – that was education they wouldn't get without my added paycheck. They learned to ski at Vail, to snorkel in Bermuda. I thank God every night that Bob and Tim turned out so well."

Carol frowned in self-recrimination. "I failed that course."

"Don't you ever say that!" Iris lashed at her. "You're one of the best mothers I've ever known."

"I wasn't there when Ronnie needed me. I should have been home for her. She was always pushed into after-school activities or with babysitters. Until this last year, when I told myself she was old enough to be without supervision after school. I should have been home when she came back from that last weekend with Jason! She'd be alive, Iris!"

"You didn't fail Ronnie in any way," Iris said with calculated calm. "You were a fine, loving mother. It's time you realize that giving birth doesn't make you a prisoner for life. Children grow up, marry, move away – often to different parts of the country – or stay single and get caught up in their own lives. Mothers have to learn to build lives of their own."

Carol smiled faintly. "You did. I'm not sure I can."

"Don't let Larry get away." Iris abandoned a pretense

of eating. "He's a terrific guy – and he loves you. But don't expect him to hang around forever without some hope. He went through almost six years of purgatory after his wife and child were killed. Then he met you. You're thirty-five years old – according to statistics you've got more than half your life ahead of you. Carol, don't throw those years away."

But Carol's mind was darting back through the years. So many nights when she'd been riddled with guilt. Like that cold winter night when Ronnie was eight . . .

Carol gazed anxiously at Ronnie while they sat at dinner. "You're not eating much. Did you stuff yourself with cookies this afternoon?"

"I'm not hungry." Ronnie put down her fork.

"But you love spaghetti," Carol reproached. *Is she coming down with something? Colds and viruses are going around like crazy.*

"I just want to go to sleep." Ronnie pushed back her chair, then sneezed. "I don't feel good."

"You're coming down with a cold." Carol left her chair to cross to Ronnie. *Is she running a temperature?* Carol felt her forehead. Slightly warm, no temperature. "Have a tall glass of orange juice," she ordered, going to the refrigerator. "Then I'll tuck you in for the night. You'll feel better in the morning."

But in the morning Ronnie showed every evidence of a full-blown cold. That meant no school today – always a traumatic moment. While Ronnie lingered in bed, Carol went through the numbers she had for possible babysitters. She made the calls but nobody was available. *I have to go in to the office today – my boards are shipping. I screw up, Max will fire me.*

She couldn't send Ronnie to school with a bad cold. The nurse would send her home. Nor could she stay home because her child had a cold.

She left Ronnie – in nightie and robe and warm slippers – in front of the television, with orders to drink orange juice at regular intervals.

"I'll call you every hour, baby," she promised, feeling the worst of villains. She needed her job. She and Ronnie couldn't live on the three hundred dollars of child support Jason provided.

Carol made sure that Ronnie – who was sniffling and unhappy – double-locked the door then headed for the elevator. The sound of the television filtered from the living room. The last-choice babysitter, Carol taunted herself. But she'd call every hour, grab a cab home at lunch time. *And please God, don't let me get stuck late at the office tonight . . .*

In some ways, Ronnie had grown up too fast, Carol rebuked herself. But what had been the alternative? To go on welfare?

I should have stayed with Jason. Ronnie should have had two parents.

Fourteen

By early the following week an unseasonable heat wave had settled over Manhattan, though gathering clouds suggested that it would be transitory. In a posh thirty-fourth-floor office that looked out upon a landscaped terrace Jenkins leaned back in a leather-upholstered armchair with a contrived air of detachment.

Leon Barstow, the guru of AMO, was perspiring profusely in his Brooks Brothers suit despite the air-conditioning.

"Lieutenant, you're asking me to break a confidence as inviolate as that of a physician or a psychiatrist!" Barstow protested.

"A young girl has been murdered, Mr Barstow," Jenkins reminded. "She was involved with your group." He had been annoyed when Evans brought in the PI, but at least Henderson was bright enough to make his client come clean about the AMO business. But so far they'd come up with nothing. He needed names.

"To reveal the identities of the one hundred and ninety-nine members of that training session would be breaking the trust. It could destroy our organization. Our attorneys won't allow me to make such a disclosure." Barstow exuded an aura of intractability, but the son of a bitch knew he'd have to knuckle down eventually. "What could that list possibly tell you?" he blustered.

"It might tell us who murdered Ronnie Evans." Jenkins's eyes held Barstow's. "I'd prefer to do this *with* your cooperation."

Barstow was shuddering at the prospect of losing some of those trainees, who were bringing roughly sixty thousand dollars a week into the AMO coffers. He was worried about losing the post-graduate students and the army of volunteer helpers – an estimated five thousand unpaid zealots at his disposal. Jenkins had done extensive homework. He knew about the four thousand dollar a month apartment that was Barstow's New York pied-a-terre. He'd discovered the pertinent details of the lush Connecticut estate furnished with authentic antiques and providing theater, greenhouse and indoor heated pool, where Barstow spent a segment of every week.

"I do this with painful reluctance." Barstow sighed and pushed a button on his desk. He leaned back with an air of weariness.

The door opened. A stern-faced, middle-aged woman with guarded eyes came into the office, closed the door behind her. Jenkins intercepted the silent exchange between them. This woman was no volunteer.

"Gertrude, will you please take Lieutenant Jenkins into your office and provide him with the information he requests."

This was Gertrude March, Jenkins's mind registered, Barstow's business manager and constant companion. He realized now that the March woman had been listening in to their conversation through the intercom on Barstow's desk.

In a small, austere office to the left of Barstow's his business manger laid before Jenkins the book that listed the names of those enrolled in Ronnie's training. He suppressed his astonishment when he recognized some of those names.

"I hope you'll explain to whomever you question that the revelation of their enrollment was given under duress," Gertrude March said coldly. She hesitated. "You won't question all of them?"

"Just four," Jenkins reassured, making notes in his small, precise handwriting. They were all here – the names Ronnie had listed. Charles, Douglas, Anthony, Amelia. What luck that in a group of two hundred people there was no duplication of these four names. AMO was thorough – their listing included both home and business addresses and telephone numbers. *Why had Ronnie made that list? What did it mean?*

One hour later Jenkins was sitting in Charles Reid's office, explaining the reason for his presence.

"Yes, there was a girl named Ronnie in my training," Reid acknowledged. His hand was unsteady as he reached for a cigarette, offered one to Jenkins, a non-smoker. "But I never connected her with the girl that was murdered. The newspaper photos bore little resemblance," he said with a wry smile.

"How often did you see Ronnie Evans outside of the training sessions?" Jenkins asked. He saw Reid start.

"Once," he said. "On a mid-week afternoon between the two training weekends. She asked me to help her choose a wallet for her father's birthday. We met in Saks. She bought the wallet and . . ." He hesitated, weighing a further revelation. "We had a cocktail together before I

116

saw her into a taxi. I was under the impression that she was considerably older." He hesitated again. "She came across as a screwed-up swinger."

"That was the only time you saw Ronnie Evans away from the AMO sessions?" Jenkins probed, his voice indicating calculated skepticism.

"The only time." Reid's voice was sharp. "Except for the times we ate together, with other people," he emphasized, "during our meal breaks."

Jenkins pushed back his chair. "Thank you, Mr Reid. We have to ask these questions, you know."

"Of course." Reid smiled perfunctorily.

"By the way," Jenkins said, en route to the door. "Where were you the evening of Ronnie Evans's murder? She was killed about seven o'clock on—"

"I know when she was killed," Reid bristled. "I heard it on the news. Am I a suspect?" But Jenkins was conscious of an air of confidence about him. "I was on a cabin cruiser off the Hamptons with a party of five at the time Ronnie Evans was murdered. I'll be happy to provide you with their names."

"That won't be necessary at the moment," Jenkins told him. Later he'd check Reid's alibi but he doubted that he was lying.

Waiting for an elevator Jenkins replayed the brief interview with Reid in his mind. Reid had an alibi for the time of Ronnie's death. So why was he such a nervous wreck at being questioned?

As Jenkins crossed the ground floor lobby, thunder rumbled. Lightning darted across the wide expanse of glass that faced the north. In seconds sheets of rain pummeled the streets. His eyes skimmed the lobby until they located a bank of telephones. Reaching for coins he headed for the one unoccupied phone. A salesman thrust himself ahead, settled at the phone and deposited change. Jenkins swore under his breath.

Tony Morrow was out of town on business, his secretary advised. He would be back in New York at the end of the week. Amelia Somers was not at the University. She didn't answer her home phone. Jenkins got his call through to Douglas Waterson.

Waterson was the kind of man who broke out in sweat if a cop looked at him sideways, Jenkins assessed within moments. Again, as with Charles Reid, he felt a sense of panic in the man he was to question.

"Look, so we were in the same AMO training," Waterson blustered. "What can I tell you about Ronnie Evans's death?"

"Your name was scrawled on a piece of paper that was found in her jacket pocket."

"That's crazy!" He sounded terrified.

"I'd like to talk to you, Mr Waterson," Jenkins persisted. "Either at your office or at home."

"Not at the office!" he rejected.

"At your apartment," Jenkins accepted. All the way up in Riverdale, damn it. "Seven-thirty okay?"

"Okay."

Jenkins heard the phone slam down. Waterson was badly shaken. What did Douglas Waterson have in common with Charles Reid, Anthony Morrow and Amelia Somers? Had one of them murdered Ronnie? Two of them were scared. He'd lay odds it would be a repeat situation when he caught up with the other two.

Little unconnected fragments were disturbing him. Was

there something he wasn't seeing? He should call Carol
Evans, talk to her again.

He called the magazine. When he gave his name,
the receptionist put him straight through. He could feel
Carol's surge of tension when she recognized his voice.

"Is there a new development?"

"Nothing substantial," he hedged, "but I'd like to fill
you in. I hate to impose, but may I drop by for ten minutes
this evening? Rather late?"

"How late?"

"About nine-thirty?"

Carol hesitated a moment. "Nine-thirty will be fine."

Carol Evans was a charming, bright woman. Before
this mess was over, Jenkins guessed, she was going to
be a shocked, disillusioned woman. A portrait of Ronnie
Evans was forming in his mind that bore no resemblance
to that cherished by her mother.

Jenkins cruised for ten minutes before he found a
parking spot, then left the car and sought out Doug
Waterson's apartment among the high-rises that overlooked the Hudson. There was no doorman. He rang and
waited for Waterson to speak to him on the intercom.

"Yes?" His voice sounded brisk. He had got himself
together, Jenkins guessed.

"Lieutenant Jenkins."

"I'll buzz you in."

Jenkins moved forward to grasp the knob as the buzzer
sounded. A high-rent apartment, he judged, thought there
were indications that the co-op board was cutting corners.
For example, the lack of a doorman. The wallpaper
showed signs of wear. The carpeting in front of the
elevator was faded.

Riding up in the elevator, he went over in his mind what little information he had acquired from the AMO file on Douglas Waterson. He was an investment counselor, recently widowed. He had never been in any kind of therapy before the AMO experience. What was his connection with Ronnie Evans? She had singled out three men and a woman for her memo. Did any – or all – of them have a motive for murder?

Waterson pulled the door open the moment Jenkins's finger touched the bell.

"Come in, Lieutenant," he invited with a polite smile. His earlier panic was under control. Xanax or Valium, Jenkins guessed. "Sorry to have to drag you all the way up here, but my office is bedlam."

"No problem." All right, so they were going to have to go through some chit-chat. He'd still get downtown by nine-thirty.

"Would you like a drink?" Waterson ushered him into a cluttered, colonial living room that looked as though it had been copied, right down to the artificial fireplace, from a magazine photograph. A room his dead wife must have spent years assembling, but hardly a room geared to a man's taste. Too fussy, too over-loaded. "Coffee?"

"Thank you, no." Jenkins sat in a chair that flanked the fireplace.

"I can't understand this whole thing," Doug said with an air of bravado, reaching for his pipe on the mantelpiece. "I mean, I hardly knew the girl."

"You were in the same training session," Jenkins reminded him. "She wrote your name and 'AMO' on a piece of paper. It was found in her jacket. Were you with her the day she died?"

Doug stared in shock.

"Of course I wasn't." He managed a smile of disbelief. "Why on earth would you think that?"

"A routine question," Jenkins shrugged. "How often did you see her?"

"I saw her at the training." His eyes were guarded. "No other time."

"Didn't you take her to dinner?" Jenkins probed. In truth he was fishing.

Doug hesitated. "Once at a meal break she ate with a group of us," he conceded. "At a neighborhood Chinese restaurant."

Jenkins nodded. "Besides that, you took her to dinner alone?"

Again Jenkins was aware of Doug's wariness. He didn't know how much they had learned, Jenkins surmised. He didn't want to be caught in a lie.

"We had coffee together in a cafeteria," he acknowledged. "It was a rotten, rainy night. Afterwards I put her into a taxi. I saw her at the training the next night. That was it."

"Where were you the night Ronnie Evans was murdered?"

Doug frowned, ran the tip of his tongue across his upper lip.

"I don't know exactly what night that was," he hedged.

Jenkins moved forward, watching Doug's face as he gave the exact time and date of Ronnie's death. No doubt about it. The guy was scared.

"I was at a movie." Doug seemed relieved to come up with an alibi. "Downtown." He told Jenkins the name of the film and the theater where it was playing. He even launched into a criticism of the performance.

121

Jenkins rose to his feet, thanked Doug for seeing him, and left the apartment. He'd even have time to drop in the office for half an hour or so before he went to call on Carol Evans. Corelli, a bachelor, had said he'd be at the office till at least ten. Maybe Corelli had located Amelia Somers.

Corelli glanced up with a grin when Jenkins walked into the office. The inevitable mug of coffee sat on his desk and he was digging with relish into a cream-filled eclair.

"This is what I like about you, Jenkins," he drawled with the unmistakable inflection of their superior. "Devotion to the job."

"You locate the Somers broad?" Jenkins dropped into a chair. Was Janet right? Should he start jogging? He was conscious of a faint thickening about his middle, the product of too many coffees and danishes when Corelli and he were slugging out a case.

"Amelia Somers has disappeared into thin air," Corelli said disgustedly. "But she'll have to surface soon. She's teaching a class in the summer session. How'd you make out with Doug Waterson?"

"He admits to seeing Ronnie alone once, but he's nervous as a rookie going in on his first raid."

"Does he have an alibi for the night of the murder?" Corelli demanded.

"He was at a movie. He gave me a rundown of the film. In detail." Jenkins grinned. "He said it was rotten. I think he's a closet critic."

"Which movie? I'll make sure to avoid it."

But when Jenkins named the film and where it was playing, Corelli sat up straight, frowning in thought.

"Waterson didn't see the film that night," he rejected.

"That was the night there was a fire at the Alpine Restaurant next door. Suspected arson. The theater was evacuated at shortly past five. It didn't re-open that night."

Jenkins whistled softly.

"Okay. So we talk to Doug Waterson again. Got any more of that bilge?" Jenkins pointed to the mug of coffee. "I've got time for a cup before I head over to talk to Carol Evans."

Fifteen

Carol made herself a cheese sandwich, more to prod herself into physical action than from hunger. Larry was working late. They'd have dinner around ten or a little later. By then Jenkins ought to have been and gone.

She carried her sandwich into the living room, deliberated a moment, then flipped on the radio. It was always set at WQXR for the classical music that helped her to relax. She ate without tasting. Numbed by grief, haunted by memories of Ronnie, her adored baby whom she had failed. Was Larry right? Should she move out of this apartment? But giving up this place would mean moving into Larry's apartment. *I'm not ready for that yet. First I need to know who murdered Ronnie. I won't be a whole human being again until I know.*

She wasn't being fair to Larry, keeping him dangling this way. But she didn't want to feel as though Ronnie's death had given her the freedom to marry. Was Jason right? she agonized. *Is Ronnie dead because I was a rotten mother?*

She deposited her plate in the sink. The salmon steaks would grill quickly and the salad was ready. Why was Larry working late tonight? she fretted – knowing she was being unreasonable. She dreaded seeing Lieutenant

Jenkins alone. When was he going to come up with something important? All these interviews – and no results.

Everybody thought she was holding up so well, that she was being strong. She wasn't. Larry held her together. But how long would he hang around, the way she treated him? He'd waited so long already.

She started at the raucous intrusion of the intercom. It was only ten minutes past nine; Jenkins was early. She crossed to the intercom, pushed the talk button.

"Mr Evans is here," the doorman told her. She froze with distaste. What did Jason want? "Mrs Evans?" the doorman prodded.

"Send him up, please." She would get rid of Jason fast. Or had Jenkins told him to come? All at once her heart was pounding.

She switched off the radio and walked to the door. She was holding it ajar when Jason emerged from the elevator. He stalked towards the apartment. His face was grim. He didn't speak until she'd closed the door behind them.

"Carol, the lousy cops are hassling me about that two hundred thousand stashed away in Ronnie's bedroom!"

"What am I supposed to do about that?" Rage ignited in her. One minute alone with Jason and the buried anger flared afresh.

"Stop pussyfooting around and tell them what it was doing there!" Jason ordered. "I can't afford an audit now!"

"I don't know what that money was doing there." Carol was unnaturally calm. It was her barrier against hysteria.

"There's no way that Ronnie could have been hiding that much money on her own." Jason was brusque. "You

125

were hiding it for your boss. That bastard Max. Ronnie used to tell me how you were always at the office at night with that son of a bitch, screwing around with him when you should have been home with your kid. I won't take the rap for his dirty money!"

"Shut up!" Carol said through clenched teeth. "Max is gay. When I stayed late at the office it was because I was working."

"You *know* about the money. I don't know what the hell you told Ronnie, but it was rotten to get her involved with that."

"Don't tell me what was rotten!" Carol's voice was shrill despite her efforts to stay in control. "Dragging her into the AMO training was rotten. Somebody from there may have killed her! How could you expose her to that?"

"Don't give me that crap. If you weren't out somewhere with that Larry creep, Ronnie would be alive."

"Jason, why did you come here?" She was trembling.

"I told you!" His face flushed. "The cops are asking questions about that two hundred thousand. Next thing I'll have the IRS on my back because of it. They're already claiming I owe that much in back taxes!"

"I can't do anything about that," Carol lashed at him. "We haven't filed joint taxes for years."

"You know more than you're telling about that money." Jason's face was florid. "You can get me off the hook at least on that!"

"That's all you give a damn about!" Carol shouted. "Getting in trouble with the IRS. You're not concerned about finding Ronnie's killer." Ronnie, who had adored him, was dead. All that concerned Jason was money he

might have to pay to the IRS. "Get out of here! Get out
of my life!"

"You don't care what happens to me!" he fumed.

"No. I don't care," she conceded. "I stopped caring a
long time ago."

The phone rang. Carol reached to pick up the receiver.
"Hello."

"I'll be leaving in about twenty minutes," Larry told her
with the tenderness that made life bearable for her. "Shall
I bring up ice-cream or frozen yogurt for dessert?"

"Either," Carol told him. She heard the slam of the
apartment door. Thank God, Jason was gone. "I had a
call from Jenkins. He'll be up shortly. He said he'd only
stay ten minutes."

"What does he want?" Larry's matter-of-fact calmness
was balm to her torn nerves.

"He said there was nothing substantial in the way of
developments, but he wanted to fill me in. Larry, I don't
think he'd be coming up if he wasn't on to something."

"Take it easy, honey," Larry soothed. "I'll be home by
quarter to ten."

The doorbell jarred her. The doorman hadn't bothered
to call up. Perhaps he was away for a moment.

"Larry, Jenkins is here." Urgency edged her voice.

"Was he announced?" Larry asked.

"No, but—"

"Ask who's there before you let him in," Larry ordered.

"I'll ask," she promised.

The caller *was* Lieutenant Jenkins. He walked into the
apartment with an air of apology.

"I don't have much to report," he acknowledged, "but
I felt you'd like to know what little I do have."

"Of course." Tension lent an involuntary sharpness to her voice. "Please sit down." *What has he come to tell me?* "Would you like some coffee?"

"Thank you, no." He smiled and sat on the sofa. Carol sat opposite, leaned forward expectantly. "We've tracked down four people whose first names match those on the list we found in Ronnie's pocket. All four were in her AMO training."

Carol's heart began to pound. "You think one of them killed her?"

"We can't assume anything," Jenkins cautioned. "But we're checking all of them out. I've interviewed one of the men. He admits to seeing Ronnie outside of the training. On a Tuesday afternoon during the week between the two weekends of the training. She never spoke about this to you?"

"No." Carol frowned, trying to reconstruct that week. "She was out of school by three. I got home around six-thirty every night that week, except Friday when we had an evening meeting. I never questioned Ronnie about what she did in the afternoons – she always told me." *But not always. That was clear now.*

"That Tuesday afternoon she met this man at Saks. He helped her choose a wallet. She told him it was a birthday present for her father."

Carol stared at him in shock. "Jason's birthday is in December."

"After they bought the wallet, he says he took her to a bar for a cocktail and then put her in a cab and—"

"He took her to a bar!" Carol interrupted in outrage. "She was fourteen years old!"

"She claimed to be older," Jenkins explained gently. "A lot of kids do that."

"But Ronnie had such a baby face! How could he—"

"Make-up," he pointed out.

But Ronnie and Cindy just played with make-up. She wore all that sophisticated camouflage outside.

"But about the wallet," Jenkins pinpointed. "Why do you suppose she said it was to be a birthday present for her father?"

"I can't understand." Carol frowned, her mind searching for an answer. "Oh, Paul's birthday was the Friday before . . . before it happened," she forced herself to continue. "Ronnie gave him a present. A wallet. She didn't show it to me. It was all wrapped up when she went to give it to him. She said she'd been saving part of her lunch money for seven weeks to pay for it."

She had been so touched. Now her eyes sought Jenkins. "Lieutenant, you're sure she went to a bar with that man?"

"I'm sure."

"But she was only fourteen." Carol protested, fresh rage spiraling in her. "What kind of a bar would allow her in?" Her eyes clung to his face. "Do you think that man killed her?"

"We don't know. But we'll find Ronnie's killer. We won't stop until we nail him."

When Jenkins left, Carol locked the door and went into the kitchen to prepare the salad dressing. What had happened that week before Ronnie died? On Tuesday she had met a man at Saks. She went with him to a bar.

What else happened those last days that Ronnie never discussed with me?

Sixteen

Ronnie and Cindy sat in a cozy rear booth at their favorite Madison Avenue hamburger emporium. By one-fifty the rush hour was over, which gave them the privacy they wanted.

Her eyes wide with shock, hamburger frozen midway between plate and mouth, Cindy gaped at Ronnie. "You're out of your mind! You wouldn't dare!"

"Sure I dare," Ronnie was triumphant. "I can handle it."

"Ronnie, you can't do it," Cindy protested, alarm making her voice harsh. "You'll go to jail!"

"Don't talk so loud," Ronnie rebuked. "I'm doing it already. If you blab, I'll go to your mother and tell her we've been fooling around with guys in Spanish Harlem." Her eyes held Cindy's in an eloquent threat. "You wouldn't like that."

"She'd tell my old man." Cindy shuddered. "I'd rather be dead."

"Keep your mouth shut and nobody'll know," Ronnie soothed. "And stop looking like I was committing mass murder. These creeps are asking for it. Besides, it's for Daddy," she added.

Charlie Reid was scared to death of her. The others

would be, too. She might be only fourteen years old but she could handle a big deal like this.

"Suppose one of them goes to the cops?"

"They wouldn't dare," Ronnie said impatiently. "I'm jailbait. They'd be up on rape charges. They could spend the next seven years in prison. Not to mention what it would do to their smug, middle-class lives. Cindy, they'll have to do what I tell them or they're in big trouble."

"Charlie," Cindy pinpointed. "You've got only Charlie on the griddle."

"I'll have four before the AMO training is over this coming weekend," Ronnie vowed, "without wasting time becoming a graduate student or volunteer. Volunteers work in the office or help at the training," she said with a look of disgust.

"We'd better eat and get out of here," Cindy said nervously. She ate her hamburger with none of her usual relish.

Three hours later Ronnie was on the phone with her mother. She lay flat on her back across the bed, cordless phone clutched in one hand.

"Mom, it's all arranged!" Ronnie wailed. "We're having pizza for dinner, then going to a flick."

"I don't like you going out in the middle of the week. You know that," Carol reminded.

"I did all my homework this afternoon." She had inveigled Paul down to the apartment to help her through it fast. "Look, if you're worried about my roaming around at night, I'll sleep over with Cindy. She's asked me already."

"Who else is going with you?" Carol asked. Her meaning was clear – would there be boys there, too?

"A couple of girls from school," Ronnie lied. "We're going to buy a pizza and split it at Cindy's house. Then we'll go off to the movie. It's just two blocks away."

No point in telling Mom that Cindy's folks were out of town overnight and thought Cindy was staying with her. "I'll sleep over at Cindy's. Her mother likes her to have company." Cindy was an only child, too.

"I don't know," Carol stalled.

"Mom, stop acting like I was a two-year-old!"

"All right," Carol capitulated. "As long as you're sleeping over with Cindy. But remember to take along your books and a change of clothes."

"Sure, Mom. See you tomorrow night."

Everything is working out fine. I'll go to the mid-week AMO, and with any kind of luck I'll pick up Doug or Tony. Cindy has already seen the flick – she'll fill me in so I can talk to Mom like I've seen it. Cindy won't answer the phone before eleven because we're supposed to be out at the flick, and if Mom calls after that, Cindy can say I'm in the shower. Mom knows I stay in there forever.

Ronnie tossed a change of clothing into a tote, shoved her books into her massive shoulder bag, and left the apartment to take a cab to Cindy's apartment. She suppressed a giggle. She was getting as bad about cabs as Cindy. Cindy cabbed to school at least three times a week. All she had to do was say she had a stomach ache or headache and was going to cut school, and her old lady got frantic and gave her cab fare.

Cindy opened the door with a self-conscious grin. "It's all clear. My folks cut out for Connecticut already. I'm supposed to be on my way to your place."

132

"They're not going to call tonight?" Ronnie asked warily.

"They won't dare call," Cindy placated. "Last time they did that – when I *was* at your apartment – I threw such a screaming fit when I came home that Mom called the doctor to come and give me a shot."

"My mom won't call before eleven," Ronnie decided. "By then I'll be out of AMO and can phone you. I'll check in," she promised.

"You're a kook to do this," Cindy sighed. "I'm scared."

"That's why I *do* and you think about it," Ronnie flipped.

"When are you seeing Charlie?" Again anxiety sneaked through.

"He's delivering the money on Friday afternoon at four o'clock. Because if he doesn't, he's sure I'm going to run to the fuzz and yell 'rape'."

Cindy made cold chicken sandwiches, brought out cans of coke, and they ate on trays in front of the thirty-six-inch color TV in the den. Moments before Ronnie was to leave for the mid-week training the telephone rang. Cindy hesitated, then reached for the den extension.

"If it's your folks, say we're just leaving for the movies," Ronnie whispered.

"Hello," Cindy said and frowned. "What's the matter, Mom?" she demanded. "I was just on my way out the door!" She pantomimed her impatience. "Yeah, I know. Make sure Carol locks the door to the terrace." She shook her head in frustration, listening to her mother's exhortations at the other end of the line. "Mom, it'd take Spider Man to climb onto that terrace."

Ronnie prepared to leave. She was wearing her Calvin Klein jeans, a skin-tight western shirt, four-inch-high backless shoes, and a make-up job that made her look a sultry nineteen. Making sure Cindy's mother heard her voice in the background, she tiptoed out of the den.

She arrived at the ballroom early. Only a few people had preceded her. Others were straggling in now. Crazy, she thought with distaste, watching the extravagant greetings on all sides. All that hugging and kissing. God, they acted like this was a family reunion!

Ronnie kept her eyes on the door. She'd bet Charlie wasn't coming to the mid-week training. Amelia was here already, looking tense and self-conscious. Ronnie smiled sweetly and lifted a hand in greeting. Tony came in and sat beside her. She saw the way his eyes followed the length of her body in the snug-fitting western shirt and jeans. He had been looking at her that way since he sat next to her on Sunday.

Tony was a corporate executive with a big house out in Westport, an estranged wife with an obsession for shopping, two kids in college and one headed there in another year. Her mind replayed his desperation-laced sharing: *I'm supposed to have it made. I earn almost two hundred thousand a year before taxes, plus all the fringe benefits. Company car, expense accounts, the usual jazz. But I've spent fourteen thousand dollars in the last twelve months on therapy, and still nothing's right.*

Tony could raise the money with no sweat. He might be all screwed up and scared to death his wife was going to walk out on him, but he looked at *her* and got turned on. That made him Target Number Two.

The room was filling up. No sign of Charlie. He had

other problems right now. Doug came in and sat behind her, to her right. She turned slightly and gave him a sympathetic smile. Everybody seemed so uptight. It was wild the way they lapped up the garbage the trainer handed out.

Volunteers snapped to attention at a signal. The doors were shut tight. Ronnie was conscious, again, of a faintly disturbing claustrophobia. But this mid-week optional session would be over at ten sharp.

"This is such shit," Tony said under his breath to the man on his right. "I don't know why the hell I came back."

"Why did you?" the other man countered with a gleam of interest in his eyes.

"It's compulsive," Tony admitted. "I've got to know how it all comes out."

"I couldn't sleep all week," Ronnie said softly. She had heard somebody else say that when she first came into the ballroom tonight. "I couldn't eat. I must have lost five pounds."

"Don't lose any more," Tony warned. "You're perfect just the way you are."

The trainer moved into position. Ronnie clenched her teeth, gearing herself to endure the next two hours. Tony was right – it was all a crock of shit. They'd have to sit here and listen to more gut-spilling that added up to nothing.

A tall, heavy woman with a face devoid of make-up, a messianic glow about her, rose to her feet to announce that since beginning the training she had been able to call her mother, to whom she had not spoken in eight years.

A man announced that he had acquired the courage

to quit the job he'd hated for twelve years. Listening to the aging elevator operator talk about his newly acquired freedom, Ronnie wondered where he would find another job. He sure as hell couldn't live on *Amo, amas, amat*.

Not everybody had optimistic reports. A woman on pills had gone through a bad scene. A man long nurtured by AA confessed he had refrained from calling for the available help and had drunk himself into a stupor from which he was only now emerging.

The trainer announced that they were able to begin a new journey. Ronnie molded her face into the acceptable attentiveness. Covertly she watched Tony. He was fed up with this whole routine. He knew it wasn't getting him anywhere. He looked more depressed than when he came in.

Ronnie was relieved when the session was over. She heard the long, shuddering sigh that involuntarily escaped Tony.

"Wasn't that a nightmare?" she whispered, her eyes telling him that he and she alone recognized the futility of this venture.

"A nightmare," he conceded, his eyes appraising.

"It's just so awfully depressing," Ronnie confided. "I wish I hadn't come tonight."

"I know." He seemed to be weighing her up. "It's still early. Why don't we go somewhere for coffee and a sandwich? It'll do us both good to talk about this crap."

"Okay," she agreed after feigned hesitancy. "In the coffee shop here?"

"Why not?" he approved.

Ronnie and Tony went into the darkly paneled, over-priced coffee shop, not surprised to find that others from the training session were gathering there in similar fashion. Tony spied a corner booth, propelled Ronnie in its direction.

A waiter came over. They ordered. Under the table his knee brushed hers. Just for a moment. Had she imagined it? No, there it was again.

"You live in Manhattan?" Tony asked.

"Yeah. East Sixties." Cindy lived in the East Sixties.

"I wish to hell I didn't have to make that trek up to Westport. I'm so damned tired of the lousy commute."

"I hated Connecticut," Ronnie shuddered.

"You lived in Connecticut?" He lifted one eyebrow. Under the table his knee pressed against hers. Unmistakable this time.

"Years ago," she dismissed, "when I was a little kid. Commuting must be an awful drag."

"The company keeps a condo here in town. I use that when I can't face the train or the long drive out to Westport." His eyes held hers. "It's a great apartment. Fantastic views. Cost the company a mint, but it's a tax write-off." He smiled. "You might get a kick out of seeing it." He made it sound spontaneous. "It's like something out of a Hollywood movie. Want to take a run up now?"

"Are you sure nobody's using it tonight?" Ronnie pretended to be indecisive. It was working out as if she had written the script herself.

"Nobody's there," he said with conviction.

"I'd love to see it," she bubbled. "After we've had our coffee."

While they ate, he told her what a rotten life he had with his wife. "All she gives a damn about are her clubs and the house. She does me a favor when she lets me into her bed," he said bitterly. "We haven't shared a room in six years."

"That's rough, Tony." Ronnie oozed sympathy. "I mean, a good-looking, macho guy like you . . ."

"I can't afford to allow her to divorce me," he said quickly. "I'm up for a vice-presidency. My boss is dyed-in-the-wool Catholic. Even a rumor of divorce would cost me the next promotion and I've worked my ass off for that. I have to admit, Sandra's great as the corporate executive's wife. She plays the game to the hilt."

"But you need some consoling when the going gets rough," Ronnie cooed.

Tony paid the check with his credit card. A major problem was solved – she knew his last name was Morrow.

They left the coffee shop and took a taxi to the corporate apartment, which overlooked the East River in the Sixties. The furniture was stark modern, the white and beige decor depressingly bland to Ronnie. All that money and they couldn't come up with something better than this?

"What'll you drink?" Tony was heading for the starkly modern bar.

"Coke, if you have it. Liquor makes me sleepy." Ronnie's smile was calculatedly sexy. "We don't want that to happen."

"No way." He grinned, loosening his tie.

"Is it okay if I call my roommate?" Ronnie asked.

"Sure, go ahead." He pointed to the telephone.

Ronnie crossed to the phone and called Cindy. Tony was whistling as he fixed himself a drink, then pulled a coke from the bar refrigerator for Ronnie. He figured her for a swinging college student or career girl, Ronnie guessed.

"Cindy, I may be late," she said, knowing that Cindy was noting the phone number on the caller ID. "See you later." Her gaze moved to Tony. "Probably much later."

Tony brought over his drink and her coke, set them down on the over-sized coffee table, then went to slide a CD into place. Ronnie sipped at her coke while hard rock invaded the room. Not really his thing, she guessed, but it made him feel young.

"Take off your clothes," he said with startling brusqueness.

"Just like that?" All at once she was scared.

"We don't have to play games, Ronnie." He swigged down his drink and reached for her. His mouth was hard, bruising, demanding. *She wasn't in charge anymore.*

"Are you worried about making your train?" she taunted when he released her. Her heart thumping. This was moving too fast.

"I'm ready to stay here all night." His eyes were enigmatic. "Take off your clothes," he reiterated.

With deliberate slowness she peeled off her shirt. Play it cool, Ronnie exhorted herself. This was going to work out. But she was nervous. He strode to a foyer closet, pulled out an attaché case. Breathing heavily he unlocked the case and withdrew a length of leather. Ronnie turned cold.

"Hit me!" he ordered, bringing the whip to her. "Hit me!" he yelled again above the blare of the music.

Ronnie stumbled to her feet, grabbed her shirt. "I'm leaving."

"Don't go running away, baby," he scolded while

she pulled on her shirt. "It'll be so cool. I'll hit you, too!"

"Get away from me!" she screeched. "I shouldn't be here. I'm only fourteen! You can go to jail! I'm only fourteen!"

"Knock it off," he said with total disbelief. "You were in the training. You have to be over eighteen."

"They put teenagers in with grown-ups," she gasped, buttoning her shirt. "Call my girlfriend, the one I phoned before. I'm supposed to be spending the night with her."

"What kind of crap are you pulling?"

"I'll show you my school ID!" She darted for her purse. He watched with growing consternation. Hands trembling she brought out her ID card, extended it. "Here . . ."

Tony inspected her photo, saw her grade level. He groaned, dropped onto a corner of the sofa.

"You goddamn crazy kid! Why did you come up here with me? I figured you for nineteen or twenty!"

"I know." All at once she was in control again. She could handle this. "But don't worry, Tony. I won't tell your wife. *Not if you do just as I say.*"

"You don't know my wife," he defied.

"Sure I do," she corrected. "Mrs Anthony Morrow. When you paid the tab at the coffee shop, you used your credit card. I saw your name. You live in Westport. No sweat to find your wife."

"You rotten little bitch!" His face was white. "What do you want?"

Seventeen

Carol set the table, started to grill the salmon steaks. The yams had been in the toaster oven for an hour; she turned the temperature down to one-fifty degrees, just enough heat to keep them warm. With this done she felt tension creeping over her again. This evening had been so insane. First Jason showing up that way, then Jenkins.

Could Jason be telling the truth about that money in Ronnie's closet? That he knew nothing about it? Then where had it come from? How little she actually knew about what went on in Ronnie's mind! In her life.

She should never have left Jason. For Ronnie's sake she should have learned to cope with his craziness. *I know how rough it can be for a child when parents divorce. Didn't I go through that myself? My parents used me as a pawn, till my father walked out when I was nine and never surfaced again. And Mom dying in a bad drug scene nine months later. Thank God for Grandma, the only sane life I'd ever known – until she died. For Ronnie's sake I should have hung in there with Jason. I should have learned to deal with Jason – for her sake.*

She started at the sound of a key in the door. Normally she felt relief when Larry was here. Tonight she was troubled. How could she keep up this charade with Larry? There could be no life for them together. He wanted a real home again, children. *I'm not fit to be a mother.*

"Hi, baby," Larry crossed to kiss her gently. Always as though she was a fragile china doll, she thought.

"Dinner will be ready in a few minutes." She headed for the kitchenette.

"What did Jenkins want?" Larry followed her, placed the container of frozen yogurt in the freezer. He was trying to appear casual, but she sensed his anxiety.

She briefed him on the encounter with the detective, told him about Jason's earlier appearance.

"You can be damn sure that Jenkins and his partner are checking into Jason's finances," Larry told her. "They'll look to see if he could have stashed that money away with Ronnie. We'll get some answers on that score."

"Jason's blowing his stack about the money. The IRS is after him for back taxes." Carol paused, puzzled. "Two hundred thousand dollars worth."

"Forget about Jason," Larry urged. "He's out of your life. His problems are not your problems."

But our child is dead, and we don't know who killed her – or why. Until we get some answers he's part of my life, no matter how much I deny it.

While the salmon steaks were grilling, she brought out the salad. "Let's eat this now." She couldn't keep Larry on the hook this way. It wasn't fair to him. He'd had enough grief. And she loved him too much to wreck his life a second time.

Not until she'd served the frozen yogurt did she launch into the conversation that had been forming in her mind as they ate.

"Larry, I think it's time to be realistic. Move back into your own apartment."

He looked unnerved but Carol knew he didn't dare ask her to move back there with him.

"I know you never get a decent night's sleep on that convertible sofa. It's not designed for long-term use." Her smile was wry. "I kind of got used to it."

"Are you sure?" He was troubled. "It's not that bad."

"I'm sure. I have to get hold of myself, stop being a hysterical wreck. I lean on you too much."

"I'll be over for dinner every night." He seemed uncertain about this. "Or we'll run out for dinner."

"Sure." She forced a smile. She couldn't break it off too quickly after all their months together, all their dreams for a future together. It would take time – but it had to be done. It was the right thing to do.

"I'll stay over tonight," he said, almost defiantly. "And if you change your mind, you know I'm available."

Jason sprawled on the apartment sofa, scowling at Frank Lieberman, his accountant. Ignoring the two men, Tiger sat in the lotus position and intoned her mantra. Jason knew Frank was annoyed at Tiger's presence, but he didn't care.

"Look, you've got to get me off the hook with the IRS. What about all those terrific contacts you're supposed to have?"

"Jason, I've been telling you all along," Frank reminded, "you've been taking outrageous chances."

"You have to take chances to stay afloat," Jason said impatiently.

"You're trying to get away with too much. Why didn't you tell me about that crummy tax shelter before you got into it? I could have told you the IRS would disallow it."

"Christ, they're disallowing most of the expenses of my trips to Europe – and that was business." He twisted around to talk to Tiger. "Tiger, get me a drink."

Tiger stared reproachfully, but she unwound herself and walked to the bar.

"You want a drink, Frank?" she asked with a sweet smile. Jason knew she loathed Frank.

"No, thanks." Frank turned back to Jason. "Look, Jason, you don't have to spend three weeks at the Dorchester, in their most expensive suite, to sign up one group for Merrimac Productions. And what were you doing in Rome two months later, and Paris six weeks after that? Your bills read like you're an Arab oil prince! This year you've got to play down some of these tabs."

"Like what?" Jason challenged.

"Like some of this crap you've given me so far this year." Frank pulled a sheaf of papers from the pocket of his jacket, began to read off items.

While Tiger resumed her meditation, Jason and Frank argued item by item.

"Okay, so the IRS makes up its own rules," Jason sulked. "Who can live any more in this country?"

"They don't pay income taxes in Monaco," Tiger interrupted her meditation to contribute.

"I don't want to live in Monaco," Jason said. "I can't run a music business from there. Frank, do something."

He turned on his charismatic charm. "I'm depending on you. If you can't help me, who can?"

"What's doing with Lou?" Frank wanted to know. "Is he coming up with anything on that two hundred thousand the cops found in Ronnie's bedroom?"

"So far zilch." Jason shook his head in frustration. "Why the hell did it have to happen to me? Just when the IRS is out to screw me. I'd swear that Carol was holding that money for her boss, but she won't come clean. She doesn't care if I rot in hell."

"I've got to get back to the office." Frank pulled himself to his feet. "Stay on Lou's back. That two hundred thousand is a rope around your neck."

"I'll call him again. So far all he's doing is running up an astronomical bill for me."

On the fourth try Jason reached Lou Henderson. "What the hell's going on?" he demanded. "Why do I always have to call you to find out what's happening?"

"This is Friday," Lou said with patience. "I said I'd call you Friday night."

"So what's happening?" Jason reiterated. Tiger abandoned meditating to fix herself a drink. He gestured to her to make another one for him.

"I'm checking out that guy Carol works for, like you said. He *could* have hot money," Lou acknowledged, "but so far I can't pin it down. I'm looking into Larry Ransome's assets, too."

"Carol has to know about that money. Lou, find out who she's covering for!"

"The people at AMO are giving me a rough time," Lou said warily. "The guys from Homicide must have put a lid on—"

"Right now I want to pin down that money," Jason interrupted. "The cops have got to realize it didn't come from me!"

"I'm working on it, Jason, but it's not easy," Lou soothed. "I'll check with you on Monday. I've got a couple of leads to follow up over the weekend. Nothing definite, but something may show."

Jason abandoned the phone to stretch out on the sofa, his fresh drink in one hand. Tiger dropped to the floor and stared at him.

"Jason, I'm not getting enough plugs on the new song. It needs more promotion," she sulked.

"For Christ sake, Tiger, it's already on the charts!" he exploded.

"Thirty-eight?" she flared. "That's rotten!"

"*Billboard* says it'll reach the Top Twenty," he retaliated. "I've got enough problems. Get off my back!"

"Honey, I know what you can do for me." She was suddenly placating. "You've let this IRS crap throw you right off base. You're the sharpest operator in the goddamn music industry. Get behind my new number," she wheedled, "take out some more trade ads. Hire an outside promotion man to get behind it."

The phone rang before Jason could reply. Swearing in irritation he picked it up. "Yeah?"

"Jason, we're having trouble," his administrative assistant reported. "Are you coming into the office today? Drake Conners is here having a tantrum because we haven't set up his tour yet."

"I won't be back in the office till Monday. Tell him to be there at noon – we'll work out the whole deal. I've just got to pull it together."

"I know, Jason, but he's—"

"I don't want to talk to Drake," Jason said with finality. "You take care of it. He needs Merrimac worse than we need him. Convince him, Deirdre."

Tiger took the phone and put it down.

"Honey, you're all tied up in knots," she crooned. "I know what you need."

"I need money," he retorted. "To pay off the IRS and to throw into the business."

"Why don't we drive out to Southampton again and hole up for a couple of days?"

"Nobody's at the Hamptons this early," he objected. "It'll be—"

"It'll be fun," she finished for him. "Just us and the sun and the sand. You haven't given back the house key yet," she reminded. "He won't mind if we go up for another look. He's hoping like hell you'll buy the place."

"He's still down in Rio," Jason admitted. "Due back next week." He didn't want to think about their last weekend at the Southampton house.

"We'll pack and drive out to Southampton," Tiger insisted. "I'll pack for you," she purred.

Jason crossed to the bar to freshen his drink. Something glittered on the floor. He bent to pick up an earring. He recognized it – one of the pair he had brought back from Madrid for Ronnie. She was wearing them that last weekend she was alive. At Southampton . . .

Eighteen

Ronnie slumped on a corner of the sofa. Her face was stormy. Why had Daddy brought her home so early? On a Friday night! It wasn't even eleven o'clock, she thought with outrage. So she had to be up early for AMO in the morning – she still didn't need to go to bed at eleven o'clock!

She ought to be feeling great. Earlier today, right after she got out of school, she had cabbed over to Saks. Charlie had been waiting for her at the Forty-Ninth Street entrance. He carried a small, cheap attaché case he must have bought in a discount store.

"This is the end of the line, Ronnie." His face was grim as he handed the attaché case to her. "If you try for a re-run, I'll have you killed."

But there were stacks of twenty-dollar bills piled up in her duffel bag now. Fifty thousand dollars worth. And Monday morning she would have more. That was when Tony was paying off. Two down and two to go.

Her heart pounded as she thought about this second weekend. She had to tie up Doug and Amelia. *She wouldn't have another chance.*

Had Charlie meant that, about killing her? It was just bluff, she persuaded herself. Besides, this was a one-shot deal. To get Daddy off the hook with the IRS.

Jason yawned, punctured her introspection. "Baby, let's call it a night. I'm bushed. Rough week at the office and not much sleep. Set your alarm in case I don't wake up in time."

"Sure, Daddy." She kissed him on one cheek and headed towards the master bedroom. Was he brushing her off because he expected Tiger? No, she rejected. Tiger had a big weekend house party. "Business," Daddy had said.

She'd expected to lie awake for hours. She fell asleep within minutes.

The alarm uttered its second warning. Ronnie left the bedroom and hurried into the bathroom. Between the slits of the half-open venetian blinds the overcast sky was visible. She showered and dressed swiftly in deference to the time, yet managed the full make-up job that added five years to her age. Skin-tight, narrow-legged jeans and a big loose sweater. Someone said they always turned the thermostat down during the second weekend so nobody got sleepy. This was the Big Weekend, when they poured eighty per cent of the training down their throats.

She reached for her LL Bean jacket and shoulder bag, found a sheet of paper to scribble a note. Daddy would probably sleep till the afternoon.

She left the apartment and hurried out into the street. The city wore its early Saturday morning deserted air. Her eyes searched for a cab. She didn't want to have to take a bus. She spied a cab and her hand shot up.

Forty minutes ahead of schedule the cab pulled up at the curb before the hotel. She would have plenty of time for breakfast. Ugh, it would be hours before they'd be let out for a meal break.

She left the cab and went directly into the coffee shop where a few early diners were scattered about the room. She spied Amelia sitting in a corner booth by herself. Her face lit up. *This was going to be a good day.*

A wistful, 'little girl' look on her face, Ronnie crossed to where Amelia sat – her face burrowed in the Saturday *Times*.

"Hi." Ronnie's voice was slightly breathless. "Would you mind if I sat with you?"

Amelia looked up, startled.

"Hi, Ronnie." She struggled for a smile. "Sure, sit down."

Ronnie slid into the booth, pulled off her jacket. She glanced around at the sprinkling of men in the coffee shop. Amelia and she were the only females.

"I'd feel so yucky eating breakfast alone here," Ronnie said with an appealing air of unease. "I mean, I figure everybody knows we're here for the AMO weekend and they think we're kooks."

"I wouldn't say that." But Amelia was tense. "Remember all the celebrities who've been in the AMO training. They discuss it on the TV talk shows."

"I'm scared about this weekend," Ronnie confessed. Amelia was obviously remembering the crap Ronnie had thrown about being lonely and unloved because she was oozing sympathy this minute. "You remember how they said they were going to throw everything at us now?"

Ronnie continued. "I mean, doesn't it scare you? I just hope I get it." *She had to rope in Amelia and Doug this weekend.*

"You will," Amelia said. But her eyes refuted this show of confidence.

"It's a good feeling being with everybody," Ronnie improvised. "I've always been such a loner."

The waitress came over to their booth. Ronnie ordered a hearty breakfast; Amelia settled for juice, a toasted English muffin and coffee. Her hands were unsteady when she reached for a cigarette and lit it.

"The last cigarette for the day," Amelia strove for lightness.

"You teach, don't you?" Ronnie asked, seemingly on impulse. "At a college."

"Yes." But Amelia was going into retreat. Don't try to be personal with Amelia, Ronnie's mind warned. But how the hell was she going to get this closet lesbian to make a pitch for her? She'd said she'd just broken up a ten-year relationship. *It's too late to look around for somebody else. It has to be Amelia.*

Ronnie retreated, made a point of talking solely about herself. "I never feel comfortable with kids my own age," she said wistfully while they drank their coffee. Amelia kept consulting her watch. They had plenty of time. "I don't know why – I like people older than myself." Her smile was apologetic. She was pointedly telling Amelia she hoped for her friendship.

"We'd better go in." Amelia reached for her check.

"Yeah," Ronnie agreed.

In silence they left the coffee shop, went into the ballroom. Everybody seemed so uptight this morning.

Julie Ellis

They were all conscious that this was the important weekend, when they'd either get it or be failures.

Ronnie shifted about in the small, hard chair while the session proceeded. From the corner of her eye she watched Doug. He was watching her. Tony wasn't here. She had suspected he wouldn't be. But he'd meet her Monday morning at the information counter at Grand Central. He wouldn't dare not to.

Doug indicated that he wanted the mike. He rose to his feet to begin another tirade against his dead wife.

"All she ever did for me was to leave me the paid-up three-family house in Brooklyn she'd inherited from her folks." *That'll be his contribution to Daddy's IRS fund.* "We owned that house for years, and she wouldn't spend a cent of its income. It all went into her private bank account."

Ronnie stiffened to attention. He hadn't mentioned the money before. All he had to do was go to the bank! He'd inherited everything – they had no kids.

"It was my job to support her," Doug pursued, "but she ran my life for me! She emasculated me!" The old cry rang out in a tortured wail.

Now the trainer turned on Doug. "You're the asshole that made it that way!" the trainer barked. "You don't even know who you are!"

All of a sudden the whole approach of the training switched. With dizzying swiftness they were being assaulted with material that sounded like gibberish to Ronnie. What the hell were they talking about? God, this stuff was heavy!

After endless hours they were released to stand in line for the available toilets and then off to a quick, late lunch.

152

She hurried out, impatient to locate Doug. She spied him heading across the lobby with a bitter, creepy man of about thirty and an older man who had said he was beginning to like himself for the first time in sixty-five years.

Ronnie contrived to join in the conversation between the three men. She saw Doug's eyes light up at her presence. The four went into a Chinese restaurant Doug had discovered earlier. He made a point of taking charge, explaining to the waiter they had to be served fast and get out. He took out his MasterCard, announced that dinner was his treat. She saw his name: Douglas A Waterson. *Okay!*

Doug was aware of her interest. He was gloating about it. He was going to be a snap to nail. *Tonight*, Ronnie stipulated.

They ate and returned to the hotel, arriving just as the sky unleashed the downpour that had been threatened since early morning. The doors to the ballroom were shut behind them. The training resumed. Everybody looked earnest, bewildered, and exhausted. Earlier than usual – slightly past midnight – they were dismissed. Tomorrow was graduation. The Big Day.

Ronnie trailed at Doug's heels, aware that he was hopeful for some encounter. It was drizzling now – a cold, depressing night. She could go home in a taxi later and explain to Daddy that she hadn't seen any sense in dragging him out in such rotten weather. Besides, he wasn't expecting her to call for at least an hour or two.

"I'll never fall asleep tonight," she said to Doug, ostensibly searching the empty street for a taxi. "I mean, the training gets you so stirred up."

"I know." He was straining to make a pitch. His wife

had sure kept him tied down. "Look, there's an all-night cafeteria a couple of blocks away. Would you like to go for coffee and talk a while? I'll see that you get home all right," he promised.

"I'd like that." Her smile was dazzling.

Doug put a hand at her elbow, indicating the direction of the restaurant. He talked compulsively as they walked. He wasn't sure he was getting the whole thing, but he felt that he was expanding his horizon via AMO.

"I'm like a guy out of jail," he told Ronnie. "I've got to learn to live again."

The cafeteria was lively with customers. The piped-in music was subdued and geared to a middle-aged clientele. Corny, Ronnie thought with distaste, but Doug liked it. He was humming under his breath.

He escorted her to a corner table that offered privacy then crossed to the counter to order coffee and hot danish for them. Where did he live? She couldn't stay overnight at his place. He'd never said where he lived. All at once she was anxious about how to handle the night.

Doug returned with a tray. He liked being seen with her. She saw how his eyes moved about the cafeteria, willing the other men to be envious of him because he was here with a young and beautiful girl.

"Do you live in Manhattan?" she asked while they ate. *I can't waste time.*

"No," he told her. "Riverdale."

For a moment she felt panic. *I can't go up to Riverdale tonight. Maybe he has a car. If he does we can go to a motel.*

"It's a rotten night for driving all the way up there," she sympathized, watching his reaction.

154

"I didn't bring my car into the city," he said. "I'm stay-ing at a hotel for the two training weekends." His voice was suddenly self-conscious. "Not the hotel arranged by the AMO people. I wanted to be on my own." Private, he meant.

The atmosphere between them was electric. Doug was getting the message that she was available. He was startled, elated, and scared. Her knee edged forward beneath the table, moved against his. Her mouth parted seductively. She heard the low sound of excitement that welled in his throat.

"It's still early for a Saturday night," she said softly. "Let's go up to your room and watch some TV." Her meaning was unmistakable. He was almost jumping out of his pants already.

"Let's go." He pushed back his chair, reached to hold her jacket for her. He didn't want to waste another minute.

They went out into the deserted street, walked in the slight drizzle to the avenue to snare a taxi. Ronnie was impressed that he was at a posh hotel. That was his way of thumbing his nose at his dead wife, she surmised.

They left the taxi and walked through the lush hotel lobby to the bank of elevators. The bellhop almost tripped because he was staring so hard at her. How many times in the years he was married had Doug dreamt of doing this? For a moment she felt queasy, remembering Tony and that goddamn whip. She hadn't counted on that. But Doug wouldn't be like that. He'd be so grateful – for a little while.

In the hotel room he turned on the bedside lamp, disappeared into the bathroom, returned in moments, stripped to a robe.

"Take off your clothes," he said, reaching to switch off the bedside lamp. Did every guy say that?

"Doug, I have to go home." She pretended to be suddenly agitated.

"Honey, we just got here!"

"I have to be home in half an hour." Her voice was wistfully apologetic. "My father would kill me if he knew I was here."

"What the hell?" He reached to switch on the lamp. "What kind of crap are you throwing at me?"

"He's old-fashioned. He figures since I'm only fourteen I ought to be—"

"Fourteen?" The word was wrenched from him. "Jesus Christ, I don't believe it!"

Ronnie pulled herself up and sat crosslegged at the edge of the bed. Just as she'd thought, this was her ballgame. He listened, mesmerized, while she gave him the message. They'd been seen together by a bellhop who'd remember her; he'd seen them coming up together to his hotel room. She was jailbait. He had to pay or she would go to the cops.

Doug was foul-mouthed and furious – but he didn't dare to refuse.

Ronnie reached for her jacket and shoulder bag and headed towards the door.

"Aren't you going to find me a taxi?" she pouted.

"Find your own taxi!" He strode to the bathroom and slammed the door shut behind him.

A hotel doorman put her into a taxi. She gave the driver her destination. The drizzle had become a heavy rain. Daddy would be pleased that she hadn't bothered him. Wouldn't he?

Nineteen

With a sigh of relief Larry finished up his long phone conversation with Sentinel Copy, knowing that Richard would make sure his complicated order was properly handled. But with that off his mind he still encountered difficulty in pursuing the task before him. He stared at the blueprints strewn across his desk but barely saw them. He was troubled by a disconcerting suspicion that Carol was making a deliberate effort to cut back on the time they spent together now.

On a sudden impulse he reached for the phone. What was Iris's number? Figures jogged in his mind. He tapped them with staccato swiftness, ignoring the guilt that he might be interrupting her at work. *If she's on a writing tear, she'll let the answering machine pick up.*

"Hello." Iris's voice was brisk yet friendly.

"Iris, I'm sorry to disturb you during working hours."

"It's okay, Larry. I'm taking a tea break." Curiosity in her voice now. "What's up?"

"Could we have lunch?" he asked. "Somewhere in your neighborhood." Carol was at the office so there was no problem about running into her. "I need to talk."

"Sure." He felt her compassion. Iris knew he was having a rough time, too. "When and where?"

They settled on one o'clock at Iris's favorite health food restaurant in the area. He waited impatiently until the time arrived to leave the office then grabbed a taxi down Second Avenue. He hurried into the restaurant. Several people were in line. Iris was already there. She had a table.

"Have you been waiting long?" He settled himself at the table.

"Just a few minutes. I figured a little before one was the right time to nab a table."

For a few moments they focused on ordering. With this out of the way Larry launched into his anxiety about his relationship with Carol.

"I know she's going through a terrible period," he told Iris. No need to remind her that he had first-hand experience of similar trauma. "But I feel her pushing me away, and it scares the hell out of me. I can't bear to see her falling into the work obsession trap. The guilt trap. How do I make her understand she's not responsible for Ronnie's death?"

"Just keep telling her, Larry." But Iris's eyes were troubled. "Donna and I try every chance we get. It's so easy for her to fall into the trap. It's the single mother's nightmare: am I cheating my daughter of a whole life by being divorced? And then for Ronnie to die like that . . ." Iris gestured eloquently.

"Carol has a right to a life of her own. I'm not letting up, Iris. But I need help."

"Once the police solve Ronnie's murder, Carol will begin to relax." But Iris was not a good actress, Larry thought – she didn't believe that.

"It could be a year before that happens." He battled with a sense of futility. "Two years." Perhaps never.

"Larry, hang in there," Iris pleaded. "You two belong together. Let Carol know you're standing by for her."

"I'm doing that! But I see her slipping away from me. I'm selfish, too. I need Carol as much as she needs me. But to marry me would be an insult to Ronnie's memory – that's what she thinks." A vein pounded at his temple. "Damn it, I feel so helpless!"

Jenkins sat in the reception room of Doug Waterson's firm and flipped through the pages of *Time*. Doug had been out of town since their encounter three nights ago; Jenkins had been calling his office and apartment every few hours ever since. His administrative assistant said only that he was away on personal business and she didn't know when he would be back. But a late afternoon phone call elicited the information that Waterson had just walked into the office.

The receptionist's inside line jingled. She picked it up, communicated briefly, and smiled at Jenkins. "Mr Waterson can see you now. It's the fourth door down on the right." She pointed along the corridor.

"Thank you." Jenkins walked across the reception room and down the corridor to Doug's office. The door was open; Doug stood close by.

"I've been away on business." His voice was testy. "You might have contacted me at my apartment."

"You might have been truthful with me," Jenkins shot back.

Doug hastily closed the door and gestured towards a chair. "Truthful about what?" he challenged, but he was uneasy.

"About your whereabouts the night Ronnie Evans was murdered." Jenkins's voice was low.

"I told you! I was at a movie. Alone."

"You were not at the movie. The theater was evacuated at five-thirty that afternoon due to a fire next door. It remained closed for the rest of the evening."

Doug's jaw sagged. The color left his face. He had not expected to be caught in a blatant lie.

"All right, I wasn't at the movie." He collapsed into the chair behind his desk with an air of defeat. "Look, I was alone. Just walking around for hours."

"Who saw you?" Jenkins probed.

"Thousands of people," Doug said impatiently. "Nobody who would have noticed. Nobody who knew me."

"It's important that somebody noticed," Jenkins told him. "Where were you walking?"

"Look, this has nothing to do with Ronnie Evans's murder."

"Your whereabouts that night has to be established," Jenkins insisted.

"I'm a widower. I was . . . I was walking around the Times Square area. I was lonely. Weekends are rotten when you're alone." He took a deep, painful breath. "All right, I'll tell you. I was on Eighth Avenue," he said bitterly, "with a hooker. She knows me. I've picked her up four times now. Her name's Alice. She's a blonde, about twenty." Involuntarily he flinched. "If you want, I'll take you down there and she'll tell you." He lowered his gaze. "You won't pull her in?"

"Mr Waterson, we're not the Vice Squad." He was unexpectedly gentle. "We just want a statement."

Jenkins left Doug's office to return to the Precinct. It irritated him that Corelli and he were coming up with so many loose ends. It bothered him that the

160

two kids – Cindy Weinberg and Paul Martin – had lied to him. What the hell had Cindy been trying to tell him that he was too dense to pick up? Something about Jason Evans knowing who might have a vendetta against Ronnie. They'd got nowhere questioning Evans.

In the squad room Corelli reported that he'd still had no luck tracking down Amelia Somers. However, according to the University, she was scheduled to attend a meeting on Friday afternoon prior to the commencement of the summer session.

"Oh, that doorman who's been on vacation just got back. You know, the one who was on duty the afternoon of Ronnie's murder. He went off duty at four that day. We ought to talk to him." Corelli checked his watch. "I can't make it today. I told that character, Lou Henderson, to drop by. I want to know why the hell he's tailing Carol Evans."

"I'll go," Jenkins said. "There's a meager chance the doorman let somebody go up to the Evans apartment earlier that day."

Approaching the apartment entrance he saw a short, squat doorman who was unfamiliar to him. This had to be José, who had gone to places unknown on his vacation.

"How was the vacation, José?" Jenkins asked, smiling down on him.

"Oh, good." José grinned. His eyes were puzzled. He was trying to place Jenkins as a tenant.

Jenkins introduced himself, explaining that the police had been waiting for José's return.

"I just want to ask you a few questions," Jenkins

explained appeasingly. "You were on duty on the eight to four shift the Sunday Ronnie Evans was killed."

"Yes, sir." José was perspiring though the day was pleasant. Maybe he was an illegal alien, Jenkins surmised. *Nothing to worry about from me. I'm not with the Department of Immigration.*

"We just want to verify a few facts," Jenkins began, but the buzzer called José away.

"Just a minute," he said in apology and moved to the intercom. "Doorman." He listened for a moment. "No ma'am, the exterminator didn't come today." He returned to stand before Jenkins. "I'm sorry, sir."

"José, do you remember seeing Ronnie Evans return home before you left work the day she was murdered?" Jason had said he dropped Ronnie home from Southampton about three.

"Yes, sir," José said. "And then I saw her again about twenty minutes before I quit for the day. She was with Paul Martin and that big dog of his."

Jenkins stiffened to attention. Paul had said he was away with his family that weekend. He said they had returned an hour after Ronnie was pushed from the terrace.

"Are you sure she was with Paul Martin?" Jenkins asked offhandedly. *Why the hell had the kid lied?*

"I'm sure." José nodded. "That was the first weekend the Martins had been in town since Christmas. Mrs Martin was waiting for a furniture delivery that Saturday, that was why they hadn't gone up to their country place." José shook his head, his eyes reminiscent. "I couldn't believe it when I read in the newspapers about her being killed."

"Did anybody come to the apartment before you went off duty that Sunday?" Jenkins asked.

"No, sir."

"Thank you, José."

"You think you ever gonna find that guy who killed Ronnie?" José asked. His eyes glistened with anger. "I hope he gets the electric chair! Nothin's too bad for that guy."

"We'll catch him," Jenkins said, with more optimism than he felt.

He headed for the office. He needed to call Carol and talk with her again. He sighed. She was going to think he was hounding her.

"What is it, Lieutenant?" Carol asked, a slight edge to her voice. Had he caught her at a bad time? Or was she annoyed at these constant calls?

"Some discrepancy in the information we've collected. I'd like your help in putting it into focus. It'll only take a few minutes," he pacified. "I could stop by the office if you like." He didn't want her to get the idea that he was always running to the apartment because he had a thing for her.

"No," Carol rejected. "It's difficult to talk here. Tonight at the apartment. About eight?"

"Eight is fine." Jenkins sighed. Belatedly he remembered he'd promised Janet he'd take her to a movie tonight. But she'd been a detective's wife long enough to know that every such arrangement came with an option clause.

Jenkins phoned Corelli. Henderson had been in, Corelli reported.

"Why was Henderson trailing Carol Evans?" Jenkins asked, annoyed at this.

"Her ex-husband thinks she knows something about that two hundred thousand stashed in Ronnie's bedroom. He's sweating out a situation with the IRS."

"Meet me for lunch. At Cosmos."

Half an hour later they sat facing each other in a rear booth. Jenkins filled Corelli in on the interview with Doug Waterson.

"What the hell links those four other than AMO?" Corelli asked with an air of frustration. "We're just missing out on something. I can feel it right at my fingertips."

"Do you feel blackmail?" Jenkins squinted in concentration.

"You mean that kid was blackmailing the four of them?" Corelli was skeptical. But only for a moment. The atmosphere was all at once charged.

"She was only fourteen," Jenkins acknowledged. "The AMO training is a gut-spilling deal. The trainees turn themselves inside out. I've been reading up on it." He'd bought a paperback that painted the whole picture. "Ronnie Evans had her choice of marks."

Corelli grunted. "Can you visualize what a big-time operator could make of that market?"

"Let's try it on for size when we catch up with Tony Morrow and Amelia Somers." Jenkins felt a heady surge of fresh confidence. "You see Morrow when he comes in to his office tomorrow. I'll be at the University when Somers emerges from the meeting on Friday. Let's tie this thing up."

"We could be on the wrong trail altogether." Corelli

retreated now. "Maybe those four names don't mean a damn. Maybe the Martin and Weinberg kids or the creepy father hold the answer to what happened." His face brightened as the waiter came to their table. "God, I could eat a horse."

Twenty

Larry was conscious of a mild headache when he returned to the office after a long morning conference with a testy client. Not enough sleep, he diagnosed. How could he sleep well these nights when he worried constantly about Carol? She was running away from him, he thought in despair. She was running away from life.

The detectives seemed to be reaching no solution. Each day now was just a repetition of the one before. Though when he'd talked with Carol last night – she'd got home close to midnight – she had said Jenkins was coming over this evening around eight: "Just to clear some minor details."

For the first time in three evenings Larry had gone to her apartment for dinner. He'd tried to suggest having dinner at some quiet restaurant but Carol had said she wasn't ready to cope with that. She was drugging herself with work – the way he had done for years. Until he met her. He didn't want that to happen to Carol.

He was jarred back to the moment by the insistent ring of his private line. He reached to pick up.

"Larry Ransome."

"Larry, this is Keith Sanders." A new client for whom he had designed a million dollar house in South Salem and which was now in construction. "My wife's on my back again. There're a few details that she'd like changed. You know women," he said indulgently.

Larry listened with strained patience to Mrs Sanders's latest 'small changes'. He braced himself for what he knew was coming.

"I know this is a last-minute request – and you have other plans most likely – but I'll have no peace until Linda goes over these changes with you. What about a quick dinner at that place where we had lunch several weeks ago – it's just about a mile from the house?"

"I did have plans," Larry began uncomfortably.

"Can't you reschedule?" Sanders wheedled. "I want to get this bloody house finished. We've sold the condo in town, and the buyers are leaning on us to close."

"All right," Larry capitulated. "What time did you have in mind?"

Carol sat in Max's office and listened to him expound on why he thought a 'one-shot' on Monica Lewinsky, Linda Tripp, and Lucianne Goldberg would be a big seller.

"Max, it's all out there for people to read," Carol rejected. "Why should they buy a one-shot?"

"Because people are voyeurs," he said in triumph. "We'll work fast, get it on the stands in a week!"

The door flew open. Donna hovered there. "Carol, a call for you. It's Larry."

"I'll take it in my office." Carol rose to her feet. "I think you're off the wall on this one, Max."

"Think about it for twenty-four hours," he called after her. "We'll talk about it then."

Carol took a deep breath as she sat before the phone.

God, she missed Larry. She'd known it would be rough, but these last evenings – and nights – without him had been deadly. But she mustn't drag him down again with her. She loved him too much for that.

"Hi, Larry." She sounded almost casual.

"Honey, I've got to drive up to South Salem this evening with the Sanders. She has more 'small details' to change."

"Rotten luck," Carol sympathized, "but she's been a problem since the first day."

"I was counting on seeing you tonight."

"Don't feel guilty," she scolded. "It's part of the job."

"Promise me you'll ask Donna to come over for dinner tonight," he ordered. "You're not working late again?" he asked in sudden alarm and then continued, "No, you've got Jenkins coming over at eight, you told me. Cut out of the office at six o'clock. Order in for you and Donna."

He sounds so anxious. But better that he's hurt now than later.

"If Donna's clear," she agreed.

"I'm calling her," he warned with an effort at lightness. "I'll bet she's clear. And I'll be over tomorrow night for sure."

Five minutes later Donna poked her head into Carol's office. "We're having dinner at your place. Larry's orders. No matter how Max carries on, we're getting out of here at six."

At six sharp Carol and Donna left the office. They shopped together at the Associated's take-out department.

"I have to go home and feed Pirate," Donna reminded Carol. "If he isn't fed on time, he's at the door meowing loud enough to disturb the whole floor. I'll be at your place in ten minutes."

At her apartment Carol changed from her Carole Little pant suit into jeans and a t-shirt. She transferred the food from containers to plates, carried them to the dining table. She glanced at the clock – Donna was running late. But they'd have plenty of time to eat before Jenkins arrived.

Why was he coming up tonight? Each evening for the past week he'd checked in with her – with no real news. In a corner of her mind she heard Larry's voice: "Carol, it could take the police a year to solve the case. Two years."

Larry was upset that she'd insisted he move back into his own apartment. He was disturbed that she was working late so many nights. He thought she was doing it to avoid seeing him, her mind taunted. And on some occasions he was right. This was the beginning of their break-up. It was something she had to do – for his sake. She mustn't drag him down with her again – he'd had enough pain. *But oh, I miss him.*

While she was putting up the coffee, she heard the buzzer. The doorman reported that Donna was downstairs.

"Send her up, please."

Donna arrived clutching a box from La Delice, the great pastry shop on Third Avenue. That explained her delay.

"I know I said I was dieting," she admitted with a defiant grin, "but I figured we could go to hell with ourselves for one night." She opened the box to display its contents. Two éclairs, two danish, three ornately decorated cupcakes, plus cookies.

"You've got enough there to feed a regiment," Carol teased, trying to reflect Donna's mood.

"You said Larry loves hot danish. Serve them with breakfast in the morning," Donna flipped.

Carol paused for a moment. "Larry's not staying here now."

Donna was startled. "You two haven't split?"

"Not exactly . . ." Carol brought flatware to the table.

"What do you mean, not exactly?"

"I . . . I told him I thought he'd be more comfortable in his own apartment. You know my sofa-bed is a dog. No, I shouldn't say that – I love dogs. But . . ."

"Carol, what kind of crazy thoughts are jumping around in your head?"

"All right – I'm trying to be realistic. It isn't fair to drag Larry through my personal trauma. He's had enough in his lifetime. And I'm not ready to make a commitment. I may never be. He needs to get on with his life."

"You're not thinking straight. Larry's the best thing that ever happened to you. I've never met two people who belonged together as much as you two. I . . ."

"Donna, don't let's talk about it now," Carol broke in, fighting for composure. "Let's eat. What's happening in your social life?"

I know how Larry and I are together – but it's not to be. He's got over one terrible hurt, I'd just bring him fresh disaster. He wants a normal marriage with children. I'm not fit to be a mother. Not after what I let happen to Ronnie. I should have been here at the apartment, waiting for her – not dashing around in East Hampton with Larry. I should have allowed her to have a pup.

"Hey, wait a minute!" All at once Carol picked up Donna's flow of conversation. "What do you mean you're seeing a guy you met on the Internet?"

170

"Oh, we're just meeting for the first go-round," Donna said lightly. "Sure, I have to check him out before we move any farther. But wow, I feel as though I've known him for months. My next-door neighbor married a guy she met on the Internet."

"Donna, this is crazy," Carol protested. "It's as bad as picking up a man at a bar." But the AIDS epidemic had cut back a lot of that, she remembered Donna saying. *'How can you ask a guy to take an AIDS test before you sleep with him? Besides, it can lie dormant for ages.'*

"No," Donna said gently. "You get to know so much about a man on the Internet. I tell you, I feel as though I've known Jimmy all my life. I know about his mother and father, his two sisters. I know his innermost thoughts. He says he wants to be able to go to see his son in his soccer game, wants to see his daughter play Cinderella in the school play. He wants to make a decent living, but he'll never live beyond his financial means. It's more important to him to have time to be part of his family than to drive a Mercedes and own a beachfront house in the Hamptons."

"That could be a line," Carol warned.

"If it is, I'll know right away." Donna was confident. "He loves kids – he's mad about his fourteen-month-old nephew. He said his sister gave up her job with a prestigious law firm so she could have time for the baby. She works at home three days a week via computer, fax and phone. And those three days her mother comes over to take care of the baby."

"Donna, be careful," Carol pleaded.

"I will." But there was a new serenity about her, Carol thought. Please God, let this be real.

They had finished dinner and stacked the handful of

171

dishes in the dishwasher by the time Jenkins arrived, somewhat earlier than anticipated.

"I hope you don't mind my coming up twenty minutes ahead of schedule," he apologized. "If I get back to Queens early enough, I can take my wife to a movie she's dying to see." Carol remembered that Jenkins had a fourteen-year-old daughter. Because of her, Larry said, Jenkins felt he had a personal stake in finding Ronnie's killer.

"Do you want me to disappear?" Donna asked.

"No," Carol said sharply, and Jenkins pantomimed his agreement.

"I'll get us coffee." Donna rose to her feet with determined cheerfulness while the other two seated themselves.

"Mrs Evans, I talked with José, the doorman who just came back from vacation." Jenkins leaned forward, his voice calm, but Carol was aware of an undercurrent of excitement in him. "He told me that he saw Ronnie with Paul just before he went off duty on the afternoon she died. That was just before four o'clock," he pinpointed.

"Jason said he brought Ronnie home around three." She gazed at him, perplexed. Where was he going with this?

"Paul told us he and his mother didn't come home until around eight that evening. His mother didn't deny this. He lied, also, about not knowing that Ronnie was involved in the AMO training."

"How do you know that?" Carol demanded.

"We can't prove it," Jenkins conceded, "but it was obvious he was lying. And now again. Why was he afraid to tell us he was here all that weekend?"

"Lieutenant, there's no way you make me believe that Paul is implicated in Ronnie's murder!" Carol's color was high. "Not that sweet boy. Maybe his mother told him to say that because she didn't want him to be involved in any way . . ." Carol gestured vaguely. "But no, not Paul!"

"I'd like you to talk with Paul and try to find out what happened between Ronnie and him that afternoon."

"They were two fourteen-year-old kids!" Carol blazed. "Why are you trying to make something dirty of their relationship? And how do you know José is telling the truth?"

"He has no reason to lie."

"What about those four people from the AMO training?" Carol asked, all at once hostile.

"We've talked to two of them so far. Both have alibis for that evening."

"Why did Ronnie write their names on that piece of paper?" The words were wrung from Carol. "What was going on that we don't know about?"

"We don't know yet." Jenkins's voice was gentle. "But we have the other two to question. As soon as we locate them—"

"Are you going to question Paul?" She tried to conceal her agitation.

"Not tonight," Jenkins told her.

Donna thrust her head through the kitchenette door.

"Coffee'll be ready in a few minutes."

"I'll take a rain check." Jenkins rose to his feet.

"Are you walking over to Third Avenue?" Donna asked him.

"Yes."

"Would you mind my walking with you? I love New York, I wouldn't live anywhere else. But all of a sudden I'm scared about floating around on my own. Don't worry, Carol," she soothed,. "I'll get over it fast enough. It's just that a woman in the elevator was telling me about a friend who'd been mugged around the corner."

Not until they were downstairs did Donna make it clear that she had deliberately arranged to leave with him.

"Look, I've been Carol's friend for five years, but there are some things I can't talk about in front of her."

"What sort of things?" Damn, he'd promised Janet they'd make the last movie showing tonight.

"Could we go somewhere and talk?" She looked as though she'd hyped herself up to this, he decided. "My apartment?"

"Coffee at Cosmos," he suggested. If this was a lonely lady looking for action, he wasn't available. "It's close and not too rushed at this hour."

"Okay." Laughter in her eyes. "Though you don't have to worry about going up to my apartment. I wouldn't try to rape you."

They settled in a rear booth at Cosmos and ordered cake and coffee. What was she going to tell him? Did she know more about Ronnie than her mother knew?

"I'll give it to you straight," Donna leaned across the table, her voice low so that the couple in the next booth could not eavesdrop. "Carol always thought Ronnie was a sweet, little angel, but I saw the hell that kooky kid put her through. And ever since I've known them there's been something weird in Ronnie's relationship with her father. I know this sounds sick, but it used to give me the creeps to hear her talk about Jason. It made me sicker the few times I saw them together."

"Go on," Jenkins prodded. The hairs on the back of his neck seemed to be standing up. "You've said this much. Fill me in."

"It's not something I can put my finger on," Donna admitted. "It's a gut reaction. Ronnie hated – physically hated – every girl Jason ever went with. When she was twelve and into voodoo, she put a newspaper photo of the girl Jason was having a thing with on a voodoo doll and stuck it with pins. Not daughterly devotion. *It was sick.* I know this sounds crazy – I don't know how it fits in with what happened to her – but I thought you ought to know."

"What about her father?" Jenkins asked. "Did you get sick vibes from him, too?"

Donna squinted, weighing this in her mind.

"Yeah. Not overtly," she emphasized, "but he had a way of talking to Ronnie like she was one of his women. I don't know if anything ever happened," she admitted. "But I had this instinct that I ought to share my thoughts with you."

"I'm glad you did," Jenkins told her. "Thank you."

Driving out to Queens Jenkins mulled over what Donna had told him. How did it fit with this murder? What was it Corelli had said while they were eating lunch? "Maybe those four names don't mean a thing. Maybe those two kids – or the creepy father – hold the answer to what happened to Ronnie Evans."

He wished with a sudden intensity that he could know what had happened to Ronnie Evans on those weekends with her father. Maybe it would hold some answers – or maybe not . . .

Twenty-One

The alarm was a raucous command in Ronnie's ear. This morning she allowed it to ring for a few moments before she shut it off. She didn't care if it did wake Daddy and Tiger. But she knew that nothing short of a bomb would wake her father this morning.

She left the bed, went into the bathroom to shower and dress for the final training session. She was wired about making contact with Amelia. *I chose bad on that one. But Amelia has money. That came out in the training.*

Where the hell did Amelia teach? The name of the college came into focus. If nothing happened today, she'd have to go up to the college, find a way to trail Amelia to her apartment.

She left the apartment in the cool, gray morning. There was nobody in the street, except those coming back from late Saturday nights and creeps going to early Mass. Churning with impatience, she waited almost ten minutes before a taxi cruised into view.

At the hotel she went into the coffee shop for breakfast. A quick, disappointing glance told her Amelia wasn't there. She saw a couple of faces she recognized from the training. Everybody was uptight because this was the last day. They weren't sure they were getting what was being thrown at them.

Ronnie ordered a hearty breakfast because it would be at least seven or eight hours before she'd have a chance to eat again. She wouldn't think about Daddy and Tiger. That was all going to change, she exulted. Daddy was going to be so thrilled when she walked in and gave him the money. He'd forget Tiger ever existed. She ate scrambled eggs and satin-brown sausages with relish, all the while visualizing Daddy's reaction when she told him he wouldn't have to worry anymore about the IRS. He wouldn't send her off to that camp in Switzerland this summer. They'd go somewhere together.

The training began with a special sense of urgency. This was the final deal – unless they went on to graduate sessions. At regular intervals Ronnie's eyes sought out Amelia. Wow, that was a wired lady! Maybe she was already sorry for what she'd said in her sharing. *How do I deal?*

She sighed with relief when – after painful hours – the meal break was announced. She ate alone at a counter seat in a corner luncheonette. No way would she be able to pick up Amelia today. She'd have to cut school on Monday and track her down.

After their meal break, one by one the trainees were put through the final, esoteric rites. Ronnie participated only when called upon. Otherwise she sat tight-lipped and sullen. I'm not going to Daddy without collecting from all four of them. Amelia's going to pay off. Before next Friday.

She'd worked it out with Mom and Daddy that she would spent next weekend with him. She'd told Daddy that Mom had a weekend business trip and Mom that Daddy would be on the Coast on business the weekend after so he wanted her the coming weekend.

It was approaching three a.m. when the training group was considered graduated. A mass of earlier graduates were brought in to applaud their efforts. The trainer dismissed them with indulgent approval and a final exhortation. "If you screw up your life, blame yourself."

Fighting frustration Ronnie sought out the bank of telephones. She spied Amelia at one. She was talking agitatedly in a low voice, deliberately keeping her conversation private. At the sight of Ronnie she seemed disconcerted. She turned, spilling a sheaf of letters from her large shoulder bag. Ronnie bent to retrieve the letters, handed them to Amelia – a secretive smile on her face. Now she knew Amelia's last name. *Important information.*

"Thank you, Ronnie." Amelia mouthed the words, stuffed the letters back into her purse and finished her telephone conversation.

Pretending to be involved in her own phone call, Ronnie watched Amelia leave. Amelia Somers – that was the name on the letters. Okay. When she got home she'd check for the address in the telephone directory.

She reached into her purse for change, dialed Jason's apartment. Everything was working out just great. Amelia would have a visitor tomorrow.

"Honey, why didn't you call me last night?" Jason reproached. "When I woke up this morning you were gone already. I was worried to death."

"The weather was so rotten last night," she said sweetly. "I didn't want to drag you out. And this morning I figured you were sleeping."

"I'll be right there, baby." Jason was solicitous. "Stay in the hotel lobby."

On Monday morning Ronnie followed her usual school-day routine. But once out of the apartment the routine was shattered. She walked west to the BMT subway, took a local to Times Square and changed to the IRT. She'd hang around outside Amelia's apartment all day, she vowed. *I have to swing this deal for Daddy. The whole two hundred thousand.*

Amelia lived on West Eighty-Fourth Street in a well-cared-for brownstone with clumps of hyacinths rising from a square of earth set behind a freshly painted, wrought-iron gate. Ronnie hesitated, walked up the stoop to check the mail boxes. A swift survey showed that Amelia lived on the fourth floor.

As Ronnie hesitated before Amelia's doorbell, the door swung wide and a woman with a briefcase charged through. Ronnie grabbed the door before it could close and moved into the foyer.

She walked up the dark, carpeted stairs to the fourth floor, located Amelia's apartment, rang the bell.

"Lorna?" Amelia asked and opened the door without waiting for a reply. She gaped in astonishment at the sight of Ronnie.

"I know I shouldn't have come to you this way," Ronnie said, wistfully apologetic. "But I have to talk to somebody, and you've always been so nice."

"I have to leave for school in ten minutes," Amelia said warily, but she moved aside for Ronnie to enter.

"Amelia, I just don't know what to do. I'm scared to death I'm pregnant." Her face tightened. "I hate men. They're all so rotten."

179

Ronnie was deliberately trading on what she remembered from the sharing. Amelia had talked about being a lesbian. About the baby she had borne eighteen years ago and given over immediately to her husband.

"Ronnie, you're not sure," Amelia pointed out carefully. "There are tests, and if you are pregnant, there are clinics that'll help you arrange for an abortion."

"I wish I'd never met him," Ronnie said passionately. "I wish I'd met somebody like you." Her eyes were limpid pools of admiration.

"You should discuss this with your family." A wall was shooting up between them. No way she could get Amelia Somers to make a pass at her, Ronnie realized. *How do I deal?*

"Could I have a glass of water?" Ronnie asked. "I'm feeling so awful."

"Of course." Amelia hurried to the kitchen.

Amelia was letting the water run, probably so it would be cold. Ronnie's gaze settled on the photograph of a young girl in cap and gown. *Amelia's daughter.* She was eighteen. She must have graduated from high school last year.

Amelia's agonized sharing replayed in Ronnie's mind: "I knew when my marriage was three months old that I couldn't hack it but by then I was pregnant. We stayed together until the baby was born. My husband convinced me that I should relinquish all claims to the baby. He took her when she was five days old. His mother raised her. I never saw her again. I'd rather die than have her know the truth about me."

Ronnie picked up the small, framed photograph and slid it into her shoulder bag. *This is the schtick I need!*

"Ronnie, I really think you ought to take your mother into your confidence," Amelia urged as she walked back into the room with a glass of water. She was obviously uncomfortable in this situation.

"I will." Ronnie ignored the extended glass. "Thanks, Amelia. Thanks a lot."

Ronnie hurried from the apartment, down the stairs and into the street. An unoccupied taxi was approaching. She held up a hand. She needed to get away before Amelia discovered she'd taken her daughter's photograph.

She leaned back in the taxi and pulled out the photograph she'd hidden in her tote. She knew what she had to do now. Churning with impatience, she drew the photograph from the frame and flipped it over. *Yes*. The name and address of the photographer was on the back. She framed in her mind the story she'd give to the photographer to persuade him to provide her with Jeannie's address. That was the daughter's name, wasn't it?

Six hours later – while her mother was still at the office – Ronnie sat cross-legged on her bed, telephone in one hand, delivering her brief, prepared script to Amelia. It was like a TV movie, she thought in triumph. Why the dead silence on the other end? *The creep hasn't fainted, has she?*

"Amelia, you have no choice," she emphasized, her heart pounding. Amelia had to believe her, had to come through, or she'd be fifty thousand short on the money for Daddy. "Pay up or I go to Jeannie. The photographer was very accommodating – he thought I was delivering a hefty inheritance. I know her name. I know where she lives."

"You can't do that!" Amelia's voice was harsh with shock.

"I'll do it," Ronnie promised. "I'll tell Jeannie her

mother didn't die when she was born. I'll tell her you're a practicing bull dyke. I'll go to the college and I'll tell them!"

"I don't have that much money," Amelia stalled. "A thousand," she offered.

"Fifty thousand," Ronnie insisted. "You have it. Remember your sharing?" Again there was a heavy silence. Ronnie could hear Amelia's painful breathing.

"All right," Amelia capitulated. "But if you come to me again – if you say one word to Jeannie – I'll kill you. I swear. I'll kill you!"

Twenty-Two

J enkins leaned back in the brown leather recliner, his shoes kicked off, necktie removed. The CD player was muted, providing a symphonic background for the conversation between Janet and Kathy. He was relieved that Janet had decided against trying to catch the last movie performance of the evening. Home was a cherished oasis of comfort and peace after the frenetic pace of the city.

Janet was on her haunches pinning up the hem of Kathy's new skirt. He had been horrified when she told him what she'd paid for the skirt and blouse. His salary never seemed to catch up with inflation. But Kathy was going to a birthday party tomorrow night, and Janet was determined she would be as well-dressed as any girl there. His two women, he thought with tenderness. Both so warm and intensely feminine.

He worried about Kathy. She was pretty and sweet – and growing up. It scared the hell out of him to think of her going out with boys. They'd watched over her so carefully all these years. Parochial school, strict rules about where she could go and when she had to be home. But how could they know what situations she might walk into?

"That's about even, Kathy," her mother decided, rising to her feet with the litheness that pleased Jenkins. Janet might be pushing forty-five, but her body was young-looking. Hell, was Donna right about Ronnie and her father? How would that tie in with Ronnie's murder?

"Kathy, I don't like the blouse unbuttoned that way." Janet's voice was firm. "Maybe the top one open, but no more."

"Mom, it's the style," Kathy protested. "Everybody wears them like this."

"If it's the style to go out and drown yourself, are you going to do that?" Janet demanded. "My fourteen-year-old daughter is not going around showing everything she's got."

"Daddy?" Kathy appealed in outrage.

"Mom's right," he seconded. Long ago Janet had convinced him they must stick together in these instances. Still, Kathy knew there were times she could twist him around her pinkie. "You should hear what the rape squad has to say about the way some women dress. It's like a printed invitation." Even in their quiet family neighborhood he worried when Kathy was out after dark.

"Was Ronnie Evans raped?" Kathy astonished him with the question.

"No," he acknowledged. "And she wasn't pregnant." The autopsy had proved that.

"Daddy, are you going to catch her killer?" This was an intense, serious Kathy. "What an awful way for her to die!"

"We're trying, baby. We don't always succeed," he reminded her. "But we have some leads." Yet the hackles at the back of his neck told him they were missing something.

"It was strange," Kathy reminisced while her mother

buttoned the blouse to the top and inspected the result with approval. "The day she was killed, I was listening to a deejay show. Tiger Rhodes – that singer Ronnie Evans's father was having a thing with – was being interviewed live on the program. Tiger was saying that right after the show she and Jason Evans were flying to Las Vegas. Mom switched to the news and a newscaster was announcing that Ronnie Evans was dead. Only he said she 'fell to her death'." Kathy's piquantly pretty face was somber. "I guess they didn't go to Vegas."

What about Tiger Rhodes? They'd never even questioned Jason's girlfriend, yet now Kathy had triggered his curiosity. *Was* there anything to what Donna had told him earlier? Instinct told him Donna was not the kind to talk for pure sensationalism, yet he was reluctant to jump to an ugly conclusion. But assuming it was true – Jason was supposed to be having a hot romance with the vocalist. Had Tiger found it necessary to remove Ronnie from the scene? Had Jason Evans's daughter intruded in that romance?

Jenkins lifted himself from the recliner and strode into the den. Janet and Kathy were engrossed in wardrobe discussion. He closed the door and dialed a friend who worked at *Billboard.*

"Fred, I need a rundown on Tiger Rhodes," he said without preliminaries. "Both professionally and personally."

"I can't give you too much off the top of my head," Fred cautioned.

"I'll phone you at the office about nine-thirty tomorrow morning. Dig into the files for me, will you?"

"Call at ten," Fred amended. "Give me time to poke around."

At ten sharp the next morning Jenkins was on the

phone with Fred. He made copious notes. Afterwards he headed for the Lincoln Center Library. In the comfort of the upstairs research division that provided background on entertainment personalities, he scanned the items in the file on Tiger Rhodes. It was meager because she was just beginning to acquire some stature, but it was helpful. Leaving the library, he picked up a handful of fan magazines, went into a coffee shop to scan the material.

Jenkins nearly scalded himself with his second cup of coffee when he ran into an interview with Tiger Rhodes. Signals flashed in his head as he read. A crazy broad, ambitious as hell and with a temper to match. *Had she been at Southampton with Ronnie and her father?* Time to have a long talk with Tiger Rhodes.

Jenkins got no answer at Jason Evans's apartment, where Tiger was rumored to be staked out. He phoned Merrimac Productions. Evans's administrative assistant told him that Jason and Tiger were in Vegas for a few days but that Jason called in every afternoon about four.

"Would you like to leave a message?" the assistant asked.

"Tell him to buzz me when he returns to New York, please," Jenkins requested and left the squad room number as well as his home number.

So they finally got out to Vegas, he thought, remembering what Kathy had told him last night.

What the hell really happened that weekend Ronnie died? Evans said she had spent the weekend at Southampton with him. With him and Tiger Rhodes? Had Ronnie come home early to do her report for school – or was it something else? That was something they'd never know.

Twenty-Three

"Mom, why do I have to wait till you get home to go to Daddy's?" Ronnie complained. "I'll get caught in all that rush-hour hassle on the bus. If I leave before five I'll miss it."

"All right, but dress warmly," Carol cautioned. "It's supposed to turn cool again on Sunday."

"Okay, Mom. See you Sunday night."

At her father's apartment Ronnie paused for brief chit-chat with the doorman. He thought she was cool. In the elevator she fished in her coat pocket for her key. Mom didn't know she had a key to Daddy's apartment. He'd warned her not to tell her.

With the key inserted in the lock Ronnie froze. Daddy was home already. She could hear Tiger and him talking above the sound of the stereo. She pulled out the key, rang the doorbell.

"Baby! You're early."

"I could leave and come back later." Her eyes were suddenly stormy.

"You little kook! I'm glad you're early. Dump your gear and we'll go out to dinner in a little while."

"This early?" She grimaced. 'We' meant Daddy and her and Tiger – who was stretched out on the floor in a yoga position.

187

"Go change into something slinky for dinner," Jason ordered. "Wear the Armani."

"What's wrong with this?" Ronnie challenged. *Tiger thought she was going to take over Daddy and push her right out. No way.*

"When I take two women to dinner at Lespinasse, I expect them to look like they belong there. Tiger, get off your ass and dress!"

Yeah, Tiger was going with them.

"I'll wear my Calvin Klein," Ronnie stipulated, ignoring his look of rebuke.

"Why don't we go to PJ Clarke's?" Tiger demanded. "I can wear jeans there."

"Because I want to go to Lespinasse!" Jason was testy. "It's one of the greatest restaurants in the world."

Ronnie hurried off to the bedroom. She'd dress fast and get out there again so she could tell Daddy what was waiting for him in the duffel bag in the master bedroom. Despite her impatience she took the time to apply her make-up with the care that transformed her into a stunning twenty-year-old.

Not until they were enjoying their awesome Lespinasse desserts did Jason announce his plans for the weekend.

"Hey, we're driving out to Southampton later tonight," he said with an insouciant smile. "Surprise, surprise!"

Ronnie stared at him in shock. When would she find a chance to talk to him alone?

"Nobody'll be there. It isn't even Memorial Day yet," Tiger protested.

"I have the keys to a gorgeous house out there. The guy's trying to sell without going through an agent."

"Why don't we go to East Hampton?" Tiger pushed. "That's the 'in' place."

"Southampton," Jason repeated. "It'll be sensational to walk along the beach by ourselves. Nobody around. I want to get away. The bastard IRS is making my life miserable."

"You can get away at East Hampton." Tiger was growing pugnacious.

Ronnie watched avidly for signs of a serious battle. Let Tiger and Daddy have a real brawl. *Then Tiger won't go with us to Southampton.*

"We're going to Southampton." Jason rejected any switch in plan.

"Jason, you know what I think?" Tiger said with deceptive calm, "I think you're becoming a goddamn snob."

"You keep saying you're dying to go to the beach. We're going. If the sun comes out tomorrow, you'll get a tan," Jason pacified.

"Are you thinking about buying that house?" All at once Tiger relinquished her rage.

"If I ever get straightened out with the IRS," Jason stipulated.

When is Daddy going to give me a chance to tell him about the money? We have to go back to the apartment to pack – I'll tell him then!

They left Lespinasse and returned to the apartment. Jason sent Tiger to the bar to fix him a drink.

"Daddy, you shouldn't drink if you have to drive," Ronnie reproached.

"Don't worry, baby, I'll be sober enough to drive." He pulled her to him and kissed her lightly on one cheek. "Go change into pants and a sweater, and pack your stuff."

189

He headed for the bar where Tiger was mixing drinks for them.

Ronnie went into the master bedroom and began to change. *She had to get Daddy here in the bedroom.* Deliberately she ripped the lace on one sneaker, then with the torn-off shred in one hand she walked to the door, opened it wide.

"Daddy, could you come here?" she asked plaintively.

He came striding from the guest bedroom, weekender in tow.

"What's up?"

"I tore my shoe lace." She held up the torn-off piece. "Do you have any others?"

"No." He dropped to his haunches. "Let me see how we can juggle what's left. You can buy another pair tomorrow in Southampton."

"Daddy," she began, her voice vibrant with excitement, "I want to show you—"

"Jason!" Tiger's powerful voice ricocheted through the apartment. "Do you really expect me to take a dress along for the weekend?"

"Take a dress!" he ordered. "And a light coat to wear with it. We'll be going out to dinner. You too, baby," he exhorted, managing to tie the lace by the elimination of two eyelets. He rose to his feet and glanced about the room. His eyes lighted on the duffel bag. "Don't drag that thing along. Take the Gucci weekender."

"Daddy, I have to talk to you!" Her voice was shrill with desperation.

"Jason, I think you've flipped your lid." Tiger strode into the room. "We're just going out to the beach. Why am I packing like I'm the ghost of Jackie O? Come on, let's go."

"As soon as Ronnie packs," Jason soothed.

Ronnie pulled down the Gucci weekender, packed the black Calvin Klein pants and top along with her corduroy slacks and ski sweater, threw in some other necessities, and slammed the bag shut. She wasn't even going to be able to take the duffel bag along. She hesitated, then shoved it in a corner of the closet. Nobody was going to break in this weekend.

They went downstairs into the garage. Tiger slid into the front seat of the Jaguar while Jason opened up the trunk. He pulled out a pillow and tossed it at Ronnie.

"Stretch out in the back and sleep," Jason told her.

"Okay," she said in a little, hurt voice. They didn't want her to see them messing around in the front seat.

Ronnie dozed most of the way out to Southampton. She awoke as they were driving up a moonlit, three-hundred-foot driveway that curved before a reproduction of an English manor house.

Tiger leaned out the window and stared. "I feel like I've died and gone to England. I expect half a dozen footman to come out to welcome us."

"Nobody's here," Jason assured, parking in front of the house. "The servants are on vacation, and the owner's in Rio."

They carried the luggage into the house. A damp chill pervaded the foyer. Jason flipped on the switch. Ronnie was impressed.

"Jason, it's like a refrigerator," Tiger complained, ignoring the splendor of the house.

"The heat's on low. I'll turn up the thermostat. It's right under the stairs," he recalled. "The house will be warm in twenty minutes."

Jason adjusted the thermostat and sought out the bar. Ronnie and Tiger followed.

"I'll start up the fireplace." He dropped to his haunches before the grate which was piled high with birch logs. "Tiger, fix me a drink." The familiar order.

Tiger checked the availability of liquor and ice cubes. Ronnie slumped into an armchair before the fireplace. It was going to be an awful weekend. Tiger wasn't going to leave Daddy alone for a minute. *I have to tell him about the money.*

Tiger came over to Jason; she was carrying two glasses. *I might as well not be here.*

"Where am I supposed to sleep?" Ronnie asked.

"Any room you like, baby," Jason told her. "Sleep well. We're going to walk miles along the beach tomorrow."

She went to him and lifted her face for a good-night kiss. "Good night, Daddy."

She went into the first bedroom at the head of the stairs, slammed the door behind her. For what seemed like hours she lay sleepless, hearing the laughter from the floor below, then from a bedroom across from her own.

She came awake with a startling sense of falling through space. Sunlight was filtering through the drapes. She tossed aside the comforter and dressed swiftly. She wouldn't need a coat today, just a heavy sweater and slacks. It was early, barely nine a.m. Daddy and Tiger wouldn't be up for hours. Fresh hurt and anger surged in her. This could be such a sensational weekend for Daddy and her if Tiger wasn't with them.

She left the house and walked towards the town. She barely saw the elegant residences that lined the avenue – all sitting behind towering hedges on sprawling lawns.

She turned into Job's Lane, chose a coffee shop for breakfast.

She ate her French toast with relish, lingered over coffee.
When would Daddy and Tiger wake up? Restless, she left
the restaurant and headed back for the house. Total stillness
greeted her. Daddy and Tiger were still holed up in their
bedroom.

Ronnie trailed into the den, tried watching television
for a while, then switched off the set. She left the den
and walked to the stairs, straining for some sound from
upstairs. Nothing. She left the house again, walked down
to the beach. It was deserted except for a man with a little
girl and an Irish Setter. Ronnie stared at the dazzling blue
of the Atlantic without seeing.

Half an hour later she returned to the house. Jason was
sauntering down the stairs.

"Hi, baby, out to the beach already?" he asked exuber-
antly.

"I went to town for breakfast, and then I went down to the
beach." She was suddenly hot with excitement. "Daddy, I
want to—"

"Jason!" Tiger called from the head of the stairs. "I'm
going to fall on my face if I don't get some food."

"Come on down and we'll go eat."

Ronnie was a silent shadow through the rest of the day. At
the beach she dropped herself onto the sand under glorious
sunshine that made the afternoon more summer than spring,
and ignored the cavorting of the two adults.

At eight they left for dinner at Bobby Van's in
Bridgehampton. Ronnie wore her Calvin Klein silk pants
and top with an alpaca wraparound coat. She knew she
looked twenty, beautiful and pampered.

As soon as they were seated at a table at Bobby Van's, Tiger bounced to her feet again. "I've got to go to the bathroom."

Now. Now she could talk to Daddy. Excitement spiraled in Ronnie. She leaned forward, her eyes bright with anticipation. "Daddy, all weekend I've been trying to tell you about—"

She stopped dead in disappointment. The waiter was standing beside them, pad poised to take their order.

"Jason, we'd better wait till Tiger comes back to order," Ronnie said desperately. She *never* called him Daddy in public.

"I'll order for her," Jason dismissed this. "What do you want, baby?"

After dinner Jason and Tiger decided they wanted to go to the Driver's Seat for drinks.

"Take me back to the house first," Ronnie insisted. "I've got a headache."

"Take a couple of aspirin and watch TV," Jason soothed. "We won't be gone long."

When Jason and Tiger had not returned by midnight, Ronnie left the whole lower floor brilliantly lit, and went up to her room to bed. She heard them come in shortly. They were drinking again.

At last she fell asleep from exhaustion. She awoke at noon to another glorious day. The house was still. *They* were going to sleep all day again. *No, they weren't,* Ronnie savagely decided.

In a sheer, black nightie and bare feet, she left her room and crossed to the bedroom occupied by Jason and Tiger. She knocked. Nobody responded. She knocked again.

"Daddy?" she called plaintively. "Daddy?"

Now she opened the door and walked inside. Jason and Tiger sprawled across a king-sized bed. Tiger wore a heavy gold chain about her neck. Jason wore nothing. Both were sleeping heavily.

"Daddy!" she wailed, shaking him. "Daddy, I feel so awful."

"Hunh?" Jason came awake slowly, blinking his eyes in reproach. "Hey, what's the problem, baby?"

"I've got this awful pain in my stomach." She clutched her middle. "Daddy, it hurts so bad." Tiger was awake now and glowering.

Jason jumped to his feet. "Show me where, Ronnie." While he spoke, he reached self-consciously for the short, silk robe that lay on the floor beside the bed.

"Here," Ronnie demonstrated pathetically. "Daddy, I want to go home."

"It could be appendicitis." Jason was apprehensive, uncertain how to handle the situation.

"It's probably gas," Tiger was blunt. "Go to the toilet."

"It hurts on my side, too," Ronnie said, her eyes clashing with Tiger's. "It's probably appendicitis. Maybe I'll have to go to the hospital."

"Oh wow, is this the pits!" Tiger stared contemptuously.

"Look, get dressed and pack, Tiger," Jason told her. "We're driving back to New York." He turned to Ronnie. "If you still feel rotten when you get home, your mother will check with her doctor."

Daddy doesn't believe I'm sick.

Within twenty minutes they were packed and in the car. At intervals Jason uttered consoling words to Ronnie. *He doesn't believe I'm sick.* Ronnie slumped in a corner of the back seat. Tiger sprawled in the front.

"Hey, you know what I'd like to do tonight?" Tiger challenged Jason.

"Tiger, I've got business in town."

"You can push off appointments. Honey, you're so damn tense. You say you always relax at the tables."

"I'll think about it," Jason said after a few moments. "We'll talk later."

When I'm not around, Ronnie fumed. Daddy couldn't go to Vegas without her telling him about the money! As soon as they got upstairs, she'd corner him and she'd tell him.

In the apartment Jason shooed her into the master bedroom to change out of her weekend clothes. He disappeared with Tiger into the guest room. While Ronnie unpacked the contents of the Gucci weekender and hung them away, she heard Tiger pressing Jason to make the late night flight to Vegas.

"We can come back in two or three days," Tiger reiterated. "Honey, it'll be great for you. Don't unpack," she exhorted.

Ronnie listened while Tiger phoned the airlines. *I'm not going to manage a minute alone with Daddy. He can't wait to take me home. Then they're heading for the airport.*

Climbing into the car, Ronnie made Jason promise to phone her later. Before their flight. Then she could tell him about the money. She'd close the door to her room. Mom wouldn't hear a thing.

"Got your keys?" Jason asked as he pulled up in front of the house.

"Yeah," Ronnie said sullenly.

With duffel bag flung over her shoulder, Ronnie watched Jason pull away from the curb. She heard him speak to Tiger: "Hey baby, you'd better bring me luck at the tables!"

Twenty-Four

Throughout the morning Carol found her mind wandering from the work ahead of her to the encounter with Lieutenant Jenkins the previous evening. She'd suspected that Paul knew about AMO, had lied out of loyalty to Ronnie. But why had he lied about when he and his mother had come home from their weekend?

Jenkins was waiting to question Paul again until he could confront him with facts. What facts? her mind demanded. How dare he insinuate there was a relationship between Paul and Ronnie that she didn't know about! But there was so much she didn't know about, an inner voice taunted.

A light knock at the door brought her back to the moment.

"Yes?"

The door swung open. Donna walked inside. "We're calling downstairs for lunch. What would you like?"

"I'm not really hungry," Carol began.

"You have to eat," Donna insisted. "Turkey on rye with a little mustard?"

"Okay," she capitulated.

"Coming up," Donna flipped and left, closing the door behind her.

Moments later the phone rang. Her private line. She tensed. That would be Larry, she surmised. He hadn't called last night.

"Carol Evans." She kept her voice business-like in the event that it wasn't Larry.

"Hi, honey," Larry's voice held a note of apology. "I got home too late last night to call you." *Doesn't he know I never fall asleep until close to dawn?* "I spent hours explaining to Linda Sanders why we couldn't incorporate the changes she had in mind. Then there was a tie-up on the highway coming in. But I do have good news of sorts."

"The Sanders are going on a round-the-world cruise?" She tried for lightness.

"I heard from Kathy Beckmann. She's worked her magic again. She's found a house for us!"

"Oh?" *How can I even think about going to Montauk with Larry?*

"The people who've rented it for the past four Augusts have just canceled. It has a water view from the living room and from one bedroom. Three minutes to the beach," he said in triumph.

Carol's heart was pounding. *I can't visualize going out to a beach house for a vacation. Not with Ronnie lying in her grave.* "Did you give her an okay?"

"Sure," Larry sounded puzzled. "I didn't think we needed to go up and see it. Somebody else would probably grab it before we could get out there."

"We'll talk about it later," she stammered.

"Carol, I have to go. A conference is about to start. I'll see you around six-thirty. Shall I bring dessert?"

"No need," she told him. "I'll pull something from the freezer."

Off the phone, she sat frozen in thought. No more stalling. She had to end it with Larry. There was no room in her life for anyone at this point. Perhaps there never would be – not even for Larry. She couldn't let him go on believing there was a future for them. She didn't want to hurt him any more than she had already.

Tonight, she ordered herself. Tonight she would make Larry understand that they were never to see each other again.

Jenkins left the store where he had been examining fan magazines and returned to the squad office. Corelli was hunched over his telephone.

"That's okay, Fred," Corelli said. "He just walked in."

"I've been holed up in the Lincoln Center Library." Jenkins dropped into the chair across from Corelli's desk. "Let's go out to Southampton and poke around. I'll fill you in on the drive out there."

"I don't think the action's in Southampton," Corelli objected. Jenkins lifted an eyebrow in question. "It looks like Amelia Somers might be our baby. The University told me this morning that she's made a change in plans. She's withdrawn from teaching this summer, claims sudden illness. She's leaving town tomorrow."

Jenkins whistled softly. "So let's go call on the lady."

"Wait, there's more." Corelli leaned back in his chair, his eyes bright. "I went to the brownstone where she lives. The super was in the foyer installing a light bulb. He told me the woman in yellow who'd been walking down the stoop as I came up was Amelia Somers." Corelli grinned. "I followed her. Right to the bank."

"So what happened there?" Jenkins's voice was low but his antennae were up.

"She closed her account. She only had a couple thousand left. On the Thursday before Ronnie Evans died, she made a hefty withdrawal. Fifty thousand dollars. Cash."

Jenkins's mind catapulted into action. "Amelia Somers, Charles Reid, Douglas Waterson, Anthony Morrow," he ticked off. "At fifty thousand each that adds up to the two hundred thousand we found in the duffel bag."

"The motive for murder," Corelli pounced. "Because he – or she – suddenly realized this greedy little girl could come calling again."

"Charles Reid and Doug Waterson have alibis for that night," Jenkins said. "Did you talk with Tony Morrow this morning?"

"Morrow's in the clear. He was at a family gathering when Ronnie Evans was killed. A dozen witnesses will back him up. I've got a gut reaction that Amelia Somers has no alibi."

Jenkins rose to his feet. "Let's go visit the lady."

They drove uptown and found a parking spot on West End, left the car and walked to Amelia Somers's apartment. They buzzed her doorbell. There was no intercom. She buzzed back and they grabbed the door.

"Fourth floor," Corelli complained. "Isn't it enough that I jog six miles every day?"

At Amelia Somers's apartment Jenkins pushed the doorbell.

"Did you forget your key, Lorna?" Amelia called and pulled the door wide. She froze at the sight of them. "Yes?" Her voice was sharp, her eyes wary.

"Ms Somers, I'm Detective Jenkins. This is Detective

Corelli." Jenkins displayed his ID. "We'd like to talk to you for a few minutes."

Color left her face. "What about?"

"The murder of Ronnie Evans."

Silently Amelia pulled the door wide and gestured them inside.

"I hardly knew her," she said, her back to the door.

"Your name was on a slip of paper found in Ronnie's jacket," Corelli pursued. "You were both in the same AMO training."

For an instant Jenkins was afraid she was going to pass out.

"They're not supposed to reveal the names of trainees," Amelia whispered.

"You paid Ronnie Evans fifty thousand dollars," Jenkins said. "She was blackmailing you."

"Yes." Amelia made no effort at denial. "She came here. She threatened me with . . . with facts she had learned through the sharing in the AMO training." She closed her eyes in pain for an instant. "I never guessed the evil in that child. I had no recourse. I had to pay her."

"She could have gone on bleeding you forever," Corelli reminded. "Unless she was silenced permanently."

Amelia recoiled, her eyes dark with disbelief. "I didn't kill Ronnie Evans. Is that why you're here?"

"You had a motive, Ms Somers," Corelli pointed out. "A strong one."

"I can't kill a waterbug." She started at the sound of the doorbell, then crossed to respond.

"Of course, you weren't the only one Ronnie was blackmailing," Jenkins was deviously casual. "There were four of you – all from the AMO group. All with the same motive." He heard the click of high heels on the uncarpeted stairs. "But each of the other three has an alibi for the afternoon Ronnie Evans was killed."

A tall, slim, attractive woman, probably ten years Amelia's junior, walked into the room and stopped dead. Her eyes turned questioningly to Amelia.

"Lorna, these detectives are investigating Ronnie Evans's murder. They know Ronnie blackmailed me."

"You shouldn't have paid her!" Lorna turned to Jenkins and Corelli. "Ronnie Evans was a little monster. Whoever murdered her did the world a favor."

"We're concerned about who is responsible for her death," Jenkins pointed out. "Ms Somers, where were you on the afternoon that Ronnie Evans was murdered. It was—"

"I know when it happened," Amelia interrupted. She clasped one hand tightly in the other. "I heard the report on the eleven o'clock news that night. I was home from two that afternoon until the next day. Alone," she conceded with an involuntary glance at Lorna. They had broken up and just now reconciled, Jenkins interpreted. "I have no alibi other than that for the night Ronnie was murdered."

The three men had established substantial alibis. Jenkins exchanged an eloquent glance with Corelli, turned to Amelia. "Ms Somers, we must ask you to remain in town for further questioning. We'll be in touch."

"No problem." Amelia's voice was defiant, but Jenkins knew she was terrified.

Lorna appeared distraught. Had Ronnie threatened to reveal that Amelia Somers had a lesbian lover? That was hardly a shocker in this decade, but it was clear the two women had not come out of the closet. They were not emotionally prepared to deal with this. Amelia had been blackmailed. She was their prime suspect.

Jenkins and Corelli drove back to the Precinct, went upstairs to the squad office. They focused on pulling together what facts they had acquired.

"We don't have enough to take her before a Grand Jury and make the charge stick," Jenkins acknowledged. "But we will."

"If she tries to leave town, we'll know about it," Corelli reminded. They'd arranged for surveillance.

"We'll have to tell Carol Evans the bad news about the blackmail," Jenkins sighed. He liked her. "This is going to shake her up."

"Yeah," Corelli agreed. "But better to hear it from us than to read it in the newspapers. It'll come out the minute the Assistant DA brings in Somers."

"You suspect Somers is going to try to skip? If she runs, we can be damn sure she's guilty. We'll nail her." Jenkins frowned in thought, glanced at his watch. "Carol gets home from her office around six-fifteen, if she isn't working late. Let's run over then."

Carol started the savory tomato sauce which was Larry's favorite with ravioli, then headed for the tiny dressing room to change into jeans and a plaid cotton shirt. Tonight she had to make Larry understand that she meant to stop seeing him, that there was no room in her life for anything except work. That was the sole road to survival.

She headed back to the kitchen to put up water to boil for the ravioli. The aroma of tomatoes, garlic and onions simmering on the range drifted into the living room. She could hear Paul out on the terrace, doing his thing with the plants. He found some solace in caring for the flowers that Ronnie had liked so much.

The sharp ring of the intercom was a jarring intrusion. She crossed to respond. "Yes?"

"Jenkins and Corelli are here," the doorman told her.

"Send them up, please, José." Why did she tense this way each time they came to the apartment? It seemed they were forever coming here. Each time she hoped they would bring news of a suspect.

Carol went to open the door, waited. She heard the elevator draw to a stop. The door slid open. The two men were approaching. Her gaze shifted from Jenkins to Corelli, back to Jenkins.

"You've learned something?" As usual at such encounters her heart began to pound.

"We have a report," Jenkins confirmed. "May we come in?"

"Please. Let me turn down the heat under the tomato sauce, and I'll be right with you. The longer it cooks the better it is." *Why am I rattling away like this? What do they have to tell me?*

Jenkins sat on the love seat, Corelli in one of a pair of chairs that faced it. As always these days, the drapes were drawn tight across the width of the room, blotting out the view of the terrace. Carol returned to the living room. She sat in the chair facing Jenkins, gearing herself for whatever she was about to hear.

"We haven't made an arrest yet, but we have a suspect with a strong motive," Jenkins said quietly. All at once Carol felt giddy.

"What motive?" The words seemed wrenched from her. After all this time, answers?

"Ronnie blackmailed this woman for fifty thousand dollars."

Carol stared at him with a blend of horror, incredulity and rage. "I don't believe it! She's lying!"

"I'm sorry. The woman admitted she gave Ronnie fifty thousand dollars. That was one-fourth of the money we discovered in Ronnie's bedroom. The woman was one of those on the list we found in Ronnie's pocket. We believe each of the three men was also blackmailed for fifty thousand, but the woman—"

"You *believe*?" Carol lashed at them. She was pale with shock, her eyes blazing. "Do you have any proof? How do you know this woman isn't lying?"

"We'll check the blackmail angle with the other three," Corelli told her. "But we expect to bring in the woman shortly on suspicion of murder. We—"

"You can't do that!" A high, shrill voice galvanised them into attention. Paul Martin had come in from the terrace.

"Why not, Paul?" Jenkins appeared to show no more than polite interest.

"She didn't do it!" The spade Paul was holding fell from his hand. His eyes were agonized. "She couldn't have killed Ronnie."

"Did you?" Jenkins countered.

Paul gaped in shock. He had not realized suspicion would shift to him.

"No!" He was trembling. "Ronnie was my best friend."

Jenkins turned at the sound of a key in the door.

Larry walked in. He froze for a moment – not expecting to find the detectives in the apartment.

Carol darted towards him. "Larry, they're trying to say Ronnie was blackmailing people. All that money in the duffel bag!"

"Paul," Jenkins pursued with quiet conviction, "do you know who killed Ronnie?"

"Paul's mother should be brought down if he's going to be questioned," Larry intercepted. "Carol, call her."

Carol hurried to the telephone.

"I lied about not seeing Ronnie that day. I was scared." Paul spoke with nervous swiftness. "She called me up about three-thirty. I told her I had to walk Machiavelli. She said she'd go with me . . ."

Twenty-Five

R onnie reached for her jacket and the apartment keys.
How could Daddy be so dumb about Tiger? He was
doing anything she wanted him to do. He was a big
music company executive – how could he go running
off to Vegas that way, just because Tiger decided she
wanted to go?

Ronnie locked the door and hurried to the elevator. She
was meeting Paul in the lobby. He was the only person in
the whole world who'd listen to her any time she wanted
him to. Even Cindy was a creep sometimes. Cindy was so
scared of her folks.

Moments later Paul emerged from another elevator.
Machiavelli was straining at the leash.

"Machiavelli's in a hurry," Paul apologized. "Come
on."

They dashed through the ornate lobby and out onto the
street. Today Machiavelli was less fastidious than usual.
He immediately settled on a spot.

"Let's go up to my apartment," Ronnie urged. She
wanted to tell Paul how awful Daddy was treating her.
After what she'd done for him.

"Mom told me to give Machiavelli a long walk," Paul
rejected. "I can't come back in less than half an hour."

"So bring Machiavelli with you. He'll fall asleep, the way he always does."

They went back into the apartment house. José grinned at them. "That dog's so big you oughta put a jockey on him and enter him at Aqueduct," he kidded.

"Paul, I'm so upset," Ronnie said fiercely when they were in the elevator alone. "Daddy's acting like such a jerk. That awful Tiger Rhodes spent the whole weekend with us. My weekend," she sulked. "They dumped me early today because Tiger wanted to go to a bar."

"You said your father takes you to bars all the time," Paul chided. He disapproved, Ronnie knew. He was an awful dork sometimes.

"Daddy didn't take me this time," Ronnie emphasized. "They wanted to get rid of me."

They went into the Evans apartment. Machiavelli collapsed on the rug, settled down to nap.

"I've got something to show you, Paul." *I have to show somebody. Paul will just die.* "But you've got to swear you won't tell anybody else in the whole world."

"I won't." He was like her slave. He adored her. He'd do anything she told him. "I swear, Ronnie."

"It's in my room."

"What do you want to show me?" Paul seemed oddly uneasy.

A triumphant smile on her face, Ronnie went into the closet and pulled out the duffel bag. She unloosed the cords and dumped some of the bundles of bills onto the bed. Paul gaped first at the money, then at her.

"It's real," she assured him.

"Where did it come from?" He was terrified.

"I didn't rob a bank," she assured him with soaring

confidence. "It was a gift," she said flippantly. "From four friends I met at AMO."

Ronnie stuffed the money back into the duffel bag, returned the bag to the closet.

"Let's go out on the terrace, and I'll tell you all about it. You remembered to water the flowers?"

"Sure." It was a soft reproach.

Paul followed her out onto the terrace, his eyes full of questions. Machiavelli snored nearby. The air was drenched with the sweetness of the hyacinths Paul had nurtured in their flower boxes. He listened, horror-stricken, while Ronnie told him in vivid detail how she had acquired the money.

"It's for Daddy," she wound up, "but I haven't even had a chance to tell him." Her eyes were rebellious. "He's going out to Las Vegas with Tiger tonight." All at once her face lit up. Her smile was dazzling. "Paul, we'll go out there, too! We can use some of the money." She'd phone Daddy's office in the morning and find out where he was staying. Wouldn't he be angry when she and Paul walked into his hotel in Vegas! Until he saw the money. He didn't deserve it, the way he was treating her. "Hey, we can do it!"

"Ronnie, we can't!"

"You're always saying you're so disgusted with your mother you feel like running away. So let's go to Vegas. I've got two hundred thousand dollars. We'll take a thousand for ourselves and give the rest to Daddy when we get out there. We'll just stay for two or three days," she cajoled.

"Our mothers will have the cops out after us!" Paul protested. "It'll be awful."

"They'll be looking for two fourteen-year-old kids. With make-up on I look like twenty. We'll use phony names and say you're my kid brother. Nobody'll find us until we're ready to be found." *After I give Daddy the money.*

"Ronnie, you've flipped out."

"Paul, we're going!" Ronnie's voice soared in triumph.

"We can't!"

"You go with me, or I'll tell your mother that we do bad things together." He knew what she was threatening, even if it wasn't true. "She'll send you away to military school. You'll hate it."

"Ronnie, we can't!"

"We're going to Vegas," she insisted. Her eyes focused on a small, white, wrought-iron chair that sat against the terrace railing. She'd *make* Paul go with her, she told herself.

She scrambled onto the chair and towered precariously above the railing. "Paul, you swear to go with me to Las Vegas now – before Mom comes home – or I'll jump off this terrace."

"Ronnie, get down!" Paul's face was ashen.

"I won't!" she screamed. "Not unless you promise to go with me."

Suddenly her eyes widened in horror. "Machiavelli, no!"

The big, clumsy dog was charging towards her. He thought it was a game.

"Machiavelli, no! No!"

Ronnie's exhortations rose to a frenzied scream as the dog jumped up and knocked the chair from beneath her.

She reached out, but there was only space. She was falling over the railing.

"No! No!"

Carol stood, pale and cold, with Larry's arm around her while Paul blurted out his story.

He was talking compulsively now. Larry had tried futilely to silence him. Why wasn't Mrs Martin here? Carol thought. That woman refused to stir from her apartment until her face was a cosmetic mask, every strand of hair in place.

"It was just like I told you," Paul reiterated, shaken by the suspicion he read in the cops' eyes. "It was an accident. I didn't tell you before because I was scared for Machiavelli. I was afraid the police would say he had to be destroyed. Machiavelli didn't mean to do it. He thought Ronnie was playing. He didn't know she'd fall off the terrace."

His eyes flicked from Jenkins to Corelli. "Don't you believe me? That's the way it happened!"

In panic Paul pushed aside the drapes, darted to open the door to the terrace. "I'll show you!"

Carol clenched her hands until the nails dug into her palms. She didn't want to look out onto the terrace, yet her eyes were drawn there compulsively.

"I was standing right here." Paul's breathing was labored. "The chair was over there." He moved it against the railing. "Ronnie climbed up on the chair."

In a frenzy to recreate the scene of Ronnie's death Paul pulled himself up on the same chair. Teetered there. The doorbell rang. Thank God – Mrs Martin, Carol thought, and dashed to respond. She opened the door.

Mrs Martin came into the foyer. "Carol, what were you so mysterious about?" She spied Machiavelli. "Has Machiavelli been down here causing trouble? Machiavelli, you bad dog!" she scolded. The big dog jumped to his feet in alarm.

Mrs Martin's eyes lighted on Paul. "Paul, what are you doing on that chair?"

Simultaneously Machiavelli charged towards Paul. Larry lunged forward, clutched Paul about the waist and pulled him to the floor as the chair fell over beneath Machiavelli's clumsy leap.

"Oh my God, Paul! You could have been killed!" Mrs Martin cried out hysterically. "Oh my God!" She rushed to throw her arms around her son.

If Larry had not reacted so quickly, Paul would have gone over the terrace railing. He would be dead. Carol's eyes met Larry's in mute realization. *That was how Ronnie had died.*

Twenty-Six

At last Carol and Larry were alone in the apartment. Carol's eyes sought out the kitchen clock. It was past eight. She felt exhausted, drained by the revelations of the last two hours. She could understand the accident that took Ronnie's life but the blackmail was incomprehensible. *How could Ronnie – my sweet, precious baby – blackmail those poor people?*

"We'll have a fashionably late dinner tonight," Larry said while he tossed the salad. "Sure you don't want to start with soup? It'll just take a couple of minutes to heat up."

"I'm not that hungry." *How can we talk about such mundane things after all that has just happened?*

"Larry, those people will get their money back, won't they?"

"Sure," Larry comforted. "Just some formalities have to be taken care of first." He focused on the burnt pot that sat in the sink. "We might be able to salvage that pot – "

"No!" Carol rejected violently. The pot that had burned while Paul told them how Ronnie had died. An accident. A silly, stupid accident! *But if I'd been here, it wouldn't have happened.*

"The water's boiling." Larry pointed to the pasta pot on the range. "You can put in the ravioli now." He was talking to her as he would a small, frightened child, she thought.

"The sauce is fine. The longer it simmers, the better it tastes. I think the rolls are ready." She reached for tongs, took the rolls from the toaster-oven. With all the insanity battering her she'd thought to heat the rolls because Larry loved them warmed up, she thought in wonderment.

She set the table while Larry added croutons to the salad, brought the bowl to the dining table. Today had been unreal. She had expected to feel less tortured once she knew how Ronnie had died. It wasn't murder at all, just a tragic accident. But that wasn't closure. *How can there ever be closure?* Larry had lost his wife and child – and he had survived. How? *How?*

"That sauce smells wonderful," Larry said, sniffing with an air of pleasure.

How can we talk this way after what happened here in the last two hours? Where did I go wrong with Ronnie that she could do something so awful? "The ravioli's ready," she said, her voice strained.

She transferred the ravioli to plates, poured over the tomato sauce, carried the plates to the table. They were sitting down to dinner as though this was just any ordinary night, she taunted herself.

Larry reached for a hot roll. "Hot bread always gives me such a feeling of comfort." He spoke softly, as though fearful of saying something that might further upset her. "A sense of being home." He seemed in some kind of inner debate. "Carol, you know what happened. It's time to begin to live again . . ." His eyes were pleading with her.

"Nothing's really changed!" Her voice soared in fresh desolation. "Ronnie's gone. I'll never see her again. Never be able to talk with her. And it's my fault. I was a rotten mother!"

"That's not true!" Larry shot back. "You were a wonderful mother. You—"

"What did I do wrong? I thought I was teaching her the right values! How could she have blackmailed those people?" Carol's voice broke. "I thought I knew her. I didn't know her at all . . ."

"You did everything any mother could do for a child. You loved her. You deprived yourself to enrich her life. You—"

"But it wasn't enough," she taunted herself passionately. "I wasn't there when she needed me. All those times when I left her at home alone when she had a bad cold or virus. The times she waited for me in restaurants because I was hung up at the office. And she was scared – this small, fragile child. I know she was. I couldn't take time off to go to school events – Max would have fired me. I needed that weekly pay check! I wasn't there like a real mother." She fought for control. "I never should have divorced Jason. My parents divorced – I knew what it did to me."

"How could you have stayed with Jason?" Larry countered. "It was worse to expose her to a boozing, drug-using, womanizing father. Carol, we live in a society where many mothers – for a variety of reasons – have to raise a child alone. And most of those children grow up to be good, responsible people. It's tough, but they do it. Life is full of compromises. You did the right thing – the only thing – you could do for Ronnie." He paused. "Carol, she was her father's child. You can't be blamed for that."

Carol's mind sought to compute what Larry had said. "I never had a chance, did I? I ran away from reality. I

215

blotted out of my mind what I didn't want to see. In my mind nothing was ever Ronnie's fault. It was my fault. Or Jason's fault. Or her therapist's fault for not understanding her. But how – *how* – could she have hurt those poor people that way?"

"Carol, it's time to let go of your mountain of guilt. I'm being selfish," he admitted, "I'm not just thinking of you. I'm thinking of us. We have a right to lives of our own. We don't have to stay here in New York," he pursued, "we'll move away – go to some pleasant, little town where you won't be haunted by ghosts. I can start up a practice anywhere—"

"But you love New York." Carol gazed at him with fresh realization of their relationship. "You love your practice here."

"I can start over," he said with confidence. "I have enough stashed away to take care of us until the business is rolling again. You must let go of this guilt feeling—"

"You'd give up your practice that you love?" She gazed at him in awe. "For me?"

"Whatever it takes, I'll do. We're talking about the rest of our lives."

"Oh, Larry, I've put you through such hell." She had been so wrapped up in her grief that she hadn't seen that he was suffering along with her. "Bless you for seeing me through this."

"Carol, remember the beautiful times with Ronnie," Larry decreed. "Brush away the ugly moments."

"Yes." She felt a surge of relief that blended now with anticipation. "There were lovely times. I'll cherish them forever."

"Our time has come." His eyes caressed her. "Our second chance. Let's use it well."

·